I0761948

The Little book of

Lesser Known Monsters®

THE LITTLE BOOK OF LESSER KNOWN MONSTERS

RORY MICHAELSON

A CIP catalogue record for this title is available from the British Library.

E-book ISBN: 978 1 8381660 4 5
Hardback ISBN: 978 1 8381660 8 3

The Little Book of Lesser Known Monsters
Illustrations by Lucie Karoline©

Lesser Known Monsters®
Cover design by Dean Cole©
Illustration by Axel Toth of Urban Knight Art©

For all of the monsters and those who love them

CONTENT NOTE

No spoilers for the *Lesser Known Monsters* books are included in these stories and they are best read at any point before *The Torn Earth*.

British English conventions, spelling, and grammar are used throughout, and some colloquialisms may appear (hopefully this gives you some fun new words to use).

Warning

Includes references to anxiety, physical abuse, emotional abuse, gore, cannibalism, drink spiking, human trafficking, and death.

I

NO PLACE LIKE HOME

PART ONE

When Daniel Owens first visited Greene Manor, he'd stood before the tall, wrought-iron gates woven with ivy, grabbed ahold of his mother's hand, and wept. When she asked him what was wrong, he'd told her he was afraid; the big house was old and there were probably ghosts inside. She'd carefully extracted his hand from hers—like a soiled napkin to be discarded—and told him not to be ridiculous. His father followed this up with a cuff around the back of Daniel's head and told him boys shouldn't cry. This encapsulated Jonathan and Karen Owens so clearly that when he'd recounted it to his therapist many years later, they'd spent the next six sessions unpicking it.

Once they'd gotten inside Greene Manor, much to his surprise, Daniel actually liked it. Not only was the interior warm and welcoming, but Aunt Beatrice and Uncle Tony were much nicer than his parents. This was chiefly because they were spectacularly unaware of how they ought to behave, or at least, how the Owens thought they should. They laughed loudly, talked with their mouths full, and hugged and kissed Daniel as often as they could. Daniel looked at his parents when they did these things and watched his father's hastily averted gaze and raised chin, his moustache quivering in disdain, and his mother's thin curled lips and flared nostrils. The Greenes were 'prone to indecent behaviour,' he often heard his parents say. 'Kooks.' But they seemed perfectly decent to Daniel. What didn't seem decent, however, was his parent's tendency to only visit Greene Manor around the holidays. The Greene's hospitality meant lavish meals always perfectly cooked and with far too much food even before they hit dessert. It was after these meals his parents would explain that they needed something. Help with an unexpected bill or a sweetener for the holiday pot. The car needed parts, or the boiler has busted, and they 'simply don't know what to do.' Daniel knew it was because the Greenes were rich. Filthy rich, his father said, like that meant they deserved to have their money taken. Aunt Bea and Uncle Tony were something else other than just rich, however. They were generous. They always gave more than was asked and seasoned it with hugs and kisses that made his father stand rigid and his mother shrivel away like an impossible human prune.

Daniel was sixteen when Uncle Tony died.

A heart attack in the garden, gone before the ambulance even arrived. Aunt Bea was heartbroken. That terrible, listless sort of grief where she barely seemed able to hold her edges together and a strong breeze might blow her apart. But then, something else had happened.

Daniel told his parents that he was gay.

He'd been emboldened by the positive response from his friends at school and hoped things would go as well at home. Excited that he finally understood why he felt different from other boys, Daniel stood in the kitchen after dinner and made his announcement, his voice small and shaking. His father had been furious. His mother had cried loud and wailing sobs until eventually his father took her away whilst staring daggers at Daniel. Neither spoke to him for the following three days. They mourned more for his expected heterosexuality than they had for Uncle Tony.

Soon after, they'd set off on the four-hour drive to visit grieving Aunt Bea. The silence on the journey was suffocating. Strangely, his parents had encouraged him to bring as many of his books as he could carry, and when they had arrived, Daniel rushed to the bathroom to relieve himself. When he came out, his books were dumped on the doorstep and his parents were gone.

And just like that, Daniel came to live with Aunt Bea in Greene Manor.

GREENE MANOR WAS A PECULIAR PLACE. It only had six bedrooms, which apparently wasn't that grand so far as Manors went. There were rarely any guests, particularly now the Owens' seasonal visits had mysteriously ceased, but each room of the house was perfectly maintained. One room in particular captured Daniel's interest; a spare bedroom that had the biggest bed he'd ever seen. It was also one of the two places that Aunt Bea actively tried to keep him out of.

There and one other.

Though Daniel never wanted for anything, and Aunt Bea forced no senseless rules upon him, there was one demand. *Never* go to the cottage at the end of the garden.

The garden was vast, so it wasn't a troublesome rule to obey. But of course, once you're told not to do a thing, it becomes all you can think about, so Daniel often stared at the old groundskeeper's cottage from afar. More than once, he thought he saw shadows moving in the windows. Aunt Bea usually told him it was just the reflection of the clouds, which always seemed odd to Daniel, that the clouds would catch in the glass even on days with clear skies.

The strangest thing about Greene Manor though, was that there were no staff to speak of. Aunt Bea did everything herself. Cleaning, cooking, gardening, the lot. It must have been exhausting, but he never even spotted her doing the chores. She was always awake and smiling when Daniel came downstairs in the morning, and the kitchen sparkling clean with baked treats still warm from the oven sitting on the countertop. The only other people Daniel saw were the local grocer who Aunt Bea paid to replenish the pantry, and the stern-faced tutor she employed to home school him for his exams called Mrs Flinch. Thankfully, Daniel had been an excellent student.

At eighteen, after his exams (and some fortunate, dusty connections between the Greenes and Cambridge University), Daniel moved out of Greene Manor and into undergraduate dormitories. He missed Aunt Bea terribly, but his education kept him busy, and then so did his Masters', and then work. He visited Aunt Bea once or twice a year and continued to do so even when he moved to New York to work with an advertising company. His annual pilgrimage to the Manor was his finest therapy; it gave him time to reflect and read, and for Aunt Bea to tell him he worked too hard. He knew she was right. He had very few friends, the ones he did were really just colleagues, and his relationships with men sputtered and failed after weeks at best.

Daniel was thirty-two when he got the call. Voicemail to be exact. The Doctor explained in a measured voice that they had terrible news. Aunt Bea had suffered a massive aneurysm and died alone in the manor.

And so, one last time, Daniel travelled home.

~

It had been almost a year since Daniel had last visited Greene Manor and it was raining when he arrived. It was only two months until Christmas and his heart ached thinking of spending it without Aunt Bea. Fortunately, his employer had given him a leave of absence and agreed to send him projects to manage from home until he was ready to return. Before he'd arrived, Daniel expected to spend a few weeks wallowing in memories, but from the second he set foot in the Manor, he knew he couldn't stay long. The place was so empty without her. Dull, as if someone had ripped out its vibrant, beating heart. It was late and dark, so he kicked off his boots and squelched in wet socks halfway to the kitchen before ridding himself of the rest of his clothes, leaving them where they fell. Fortunately, the fridge was still half stocked, so he sat at the table completely naked, eating a pork pie and weeping. Then, tired, broken, and entirely without dignity, he ambled up to his old bedroom where he took a too-hot shower and slept like the dead.

Daniel awoke with a start. He'd forgotten to close the curtains last night, so the morning sun glared through the windows accusingly. Rubbing his eyes, he rolled over and checked his phone. It was almost noon. He rarely slept so well, even with jet lag. That gave him a stark pang of guilt. How could he rest so easily when Aunt Bea had just died?

He visited the en suite before liberating some comfortable clothes he'd left in the drawers. Somehow, Aunt Bea had kept them smelling freshly laundered—that brought a fresh wave of blubbering tears. After that, he descended the stairs and entered the kitchen, where the smell of freshly baked biscuits greeted him.

Daniel half expected Aunt Bea to be sitting at the table.

Instead, he found only a tray of his favourite oatmeal rounds on the countertop.

"Hello?" His voice cracked. "Is somebody here?"

Had Aunt Bea had someone helping her in her old age? The closest neighbour was twenty minutes away, and she'd never mentioned taking on a housekeeper.

Daniel strode over to the counter and picked up one biscuit, taking a bite, as if to prove to himself that they were real.

It was still warm.

Not only that, but these were the exact biscuits that Aunt Bea always made when he was a child. Just a hint of honey, a pinch of ginger, and perfectly shaped. Daniel dropped it back to the tray where it split in two. The crumbs scratched his throat as he swallowed.

"Who's here? Who did this?"

Only deafening silence replied.

Daniel's heart pounded in his chest.

There must be a simple explanation.

He'd look around the house later, but this morning he had to see the solicitor for the reading of the will. Though Daniel hadn't seen his parents since the day they'd left him here, he suspected that streak would end today. After *that* delightful reunion, he'd need to go to the funeral home. Pushing the thoughts of incredibly discreet maids from his mind, he bounded up the stairs and flung open his suitcase on the bed, carefully retrieving his least creased shirt and pulling it on before going to the bathroom to brush his teeth.

As he left the house, he never noticed that the drenched clothes he had left on the hallway floor last night were gone.

DANIEL WAS EXHAUSTED when he got back to the manor.

The cab had been late, then taken over an hour to get into town. The reading of the will had been both more surprising and awful than he'd imagined. His parents had been there, but refused to come into the room where Daniel sat until the moment the documents were opened. They looked...the same, but old. His father wore a black suit too tight around his belly, and his mother wore an ostentatious black hat that covered much of her face, as though competing in some performative grief olympics may grant her what she desired. Neither of them looked at him, let alone spoke. After the first line of the will was read, Daniel gasped, they stood and left without uttering a word. Daniel had been too stunned by the news to stop them.

Everything.

He had gotten everything.

The estate, the assets, *and* the accounts.

He was still processing it when he arrived at the funeral home.

The old mortician—who looked minutes from a coffin himself—told Daniel that Aunt Bea had been found with fortunate haste. Apparently, she'd called the emergency services before she succumbed. This, he claimed, is what made her suitable for viewing. The words the mortician used were 'not melted.' Daniel was still thinking of those words when he looked at his aunt. The sight of her tried to sear through every happy memory he had of her smiling face. He didn't want to remember her frail and grey on that steel trolley, no matter how hard the image tried to implant itself in his mind. He wanted to think of her warm and smiling, not slack features and sagging pallid flesh like wet tissue paper.

He hadn't had the stomach for lunch after that, and traffic had been terrible out of town. It was dusk when he got back to Greene Manor, and the skies were sinking to an inky black with nary a streetlamp in sight.

Daniel had almost forgotten about the morning's events until he went back into the kitchen. Waiting on the table, fully set for one, was a large silver serving tray covered with its cloche. Slowly, he approached, his eyes searching the room for the helpful perpetrator. For a moment, he envisioned lifting the bell to find a disembodied head on the serving tray beneath. Instead, when he popped off the lid, there was a freshly roasted chicken with all the trimmings.

Daniel dropped the lid onto the table with a clatter.

"Hello?!" he shouted, spinning around.

Nobody.

His stomach grumbled loudly.

He swallowed, eying the succulent meat, and then sat down and ate.

~

IT WAS the pitch of night when a strange noise awoke Daniel.

At first, he thought it was thunder. There was a deep rumbling quality to it, like a threat of flashing violence. But as Daniel listened, he realised two things. First, the rumble had a low wailing within, like the whining groan of a falling tree. Second, the noise was coming from inside the house.

Wearing only his striped boxers and white T-shirt, Daniel picked up the most robust item nearby, the glass jug of water from his nightstand, and set out to find the source of the noise.

He tiptoed down the stairs, pitcher clutched in a white-knuckled fist. When he reached the bottom that he realised he perhaps should have called the police. Yes, it might take them an hour to get here, but what was he thinking, wandering around in his underthings with only a jug as a weapon? But the rumbling sound had stopped now. If he listened carefully, he could hear a low sniffle. Like a large dog looking for a treat it knew was nearby.

Unable to resist, Daniel slowly made his way toward the sound, which came from the direction of the study.

As he got closer, his heart tried to beat its way out of his throat. He risked one more step, and the old floorboards creaked beneath his bare feet.

Immediately, the sniffling sound stopped.

Daniel froze.

He stood like a statue until his muscles ached. Then, slowly, he took a step forward and pushed open the study door.

The place had barely changed from when Uncle Tony had been alive. Aunt Bea had always talked about using it as a sewing room, but she'd always favoured doing her needlework in the conservatory. A large desk dominated the room, the same mahogany as the bookcases lining it. Daniel wished he loved the beautiful books filling the shelves, but he'd never been drawn to the classics. The only sound Daniel could hear now was his own breath, rasping in his ears as he stepped inside and the deep piled rug swallowed up his toes greedily. He tried to calm himself, to slow his heavy breath, but something was wrong.

Daniel held his breath altogether.

But the heavy, rasping sound continued.

Oh.

It hadn't been his breath. It was just so close it sounded as though it was.

Daniel twisted around.

Standing there beside the door was a man, only it wasn't a man at all.

The figure towered at least six and a half feet. Darkness masked most of it, but its long arms hung low, with massive hands big enough to wrap around Daniel's entire head like a satsuma. At first, he thought it wore a particularly loose knit jumper, but as he stared in horror, he realised it was hair. Hair more like fur, standing in coarse dark tufts all over its body, from its knuckles, up thick forearms corded with muscle, to its wide neck and all over its substantial belly.

He would have screamed—should have screamed—but there was one thing stopping him.

This vast hairy monster wore trousers. Trousers in the most vivid garish pink that Daniel had ever seen. Massive feet peeked out of the bottom with big, hairy toes.

It was absurd.

"Who...who are you?" Daniel stammered.

The thing took three long, steady breaths before it answered. The deep rumble of its voice confirmed this was the sound that had woken him.

"Knud," it said. It sounded more like a grunt than a name.

"Wh...what are you doing here, Mister Knud?" Daniel squeaked.

The thing said, "This...home."

A hysterical laugh bubbled in Daniel's throat.

One of the thing's giant hands reached up, each finger as thick around as three of Daniel's own bunched together, nails blunt and tidy. "Don't be scared...Daniel."

Daniel let out a low moan of surprise. "How do you..."

He didn't have the strength in him to finish.

"Knud always been here. Since you was a boy," the thing rumbled.

Daniel shook his head, confused. He tried to peer deeper into the shadows and see the thing's face. "I don't think so, I—"

"Knud cook and clean and keep the garden green. Knud wash your clothes and bake your loaves and always stays unseen," Knud rumbled in a low, wavering, singsong voice.

It was so strangely endearing, Daniel almost forgot to be afraid for a moment.

"Knud seen you looking at his house. At bottom of garden," Knud said.

The words were like a blow knocking the wind out of Daniel's chest. "Oh."

'Never go to the cottage at the end of the garden.'

Knud's patient, rasping breath filled the silence.

"It...it's you?" Daniel whispered. "You've really been here all these years? You manage the house? It was you helping Auntie Bea?"

The thing sniffled sadly in the shadows and let out a low grunt.

"Well, I'm very sorry, Mister Knud," Daniel said softly, his eyes travelling over that large round furry belly again. Was this a dream? "Perhaps we should discuss this in the morning?"

Daniel raised his hand awkwardly. He'd become very accustomed to the formal greeting in his business practices and handshakes had become strangely ingrained in him, but his eyes fixed on Knud's massive hand in sudden regret at his own reflexive gesture.

Slowly, one of those vast feet moved forward, and the floorboards groaned under Knud's heft as his face emerged from the shadows.

His head was enormous. At least twice the size that of any man Daniel had ever seen. His blocky jaw had a short, heavy beard, and two tusk-like teeth protruded up from his full lips. The centre of his face was hairless, a broad nose over his dusky skin. Two stout, dark horns stood from his brow amid the mane-like hair on his head. His eyes shone in a strip of moonlight, red as blood.

Daniel froze, rapt with terror.

One of Knud's hands, with its massive sausage-like fingers, reached closer to him, grasping.

Daniel screamed.

Every bit of sense fled his person, and he flung the jug he still clutched. It flew true. Careening through the brief space between him and the monster before connecting solidly with Knud's forehead with a loud thunk.

Knud's head snapped back with the impact, and the jug fell onto the rug unbroken.

Daniel's whole body shook and cold water seeped into the rug around his toes. His eyes remained fixed on Knud.

Slowly, Knud's head moved down. A rivulet of dark blood ran from his forehead from beside one of his stubby horns, meandering around one thick eyebrow to trickle down the side of his wide nose. His red eyes flashed fury, and his wide mouth bared large sharp teeth.

Daniel fled.

To be continued...

2

MEAT YOUR GREENS

Edwin Tarry was not a wicked man. He may have been described as greedy or crass on more than one occasion, but he found a good wife for himself, and together they made a steady life on Tarry Farm, where they raised their two boys into fine men.

Some local farmers were never short of gold; be it their cattle's bounty of dairy or their hives dripping honey sold in town for extortionate fees. But Tarry Farm was a modest place set between two mountains. The gravelly earth gave meagre crops, tall dry trees, and little room for livestock to graze. Despite that, the Tarry's always had *enough*. Enough to keep their backsides warm through long winters and school the boys well. Enough to get by until Edwin and Peppin spent more of their long summer days and chilly winter nights together in peace. With the boys moved away, any spare coin the farm made went into a stout pot on the kitchen shelf for a big trip that may never come.

Edwin, however, had decided some years ago that he truly *had* had enough. Enough of the arrogant pitying looks from the other farmers and the idle smiles of his sons when they came on their rare visits from the city. It was time for him to find a new life. A life full of travels and luxury, and an end to the backbreaking work on the little farm that had given so little in return. He wasn't a young man by any means, and Peppin wasn't much the adventurous sort, but he harboured the dark thought that when the money was saved, he'd find no shame in leaving his wife behind if need be. It was time to claim the life he deserved.

In Spring, once the morning's work was done, Edwin could either take a stroll and imagine his secret future or stay at the house and receive a list of jobs from Peppin. And so, it was one afternoon in May that Edwin Tarry found something strange whilst wandering behind the old sheds. Lost in a vision of a distant beach, he caught a faint mewling cry that sounded an awful lot like a lamb. A lamb where it oughtn't be, no less. It took him several minutes of searching to even consider looking in the copse that grew by the mountainside. He wondered when the last time he'd been amongst those trees had been, and as he wondered, his feet were already taking him there. But how might one of his sheep have found their way out and into the trees?

In a few short moments, he'd scoured the copse thoroughly, finding nothing of note. No sheep, lamb, nor anything else. He was just about to leave when he heard it again. The high nasal bleat gave him quite a start as it came from nowhere around him but above.

Shielding his eyes from the afternoon sun, Edwin looked up and was mystified by what he saw. High in a frail and sorry tree sat a lamb that looked barely a couple of weeks old. As if that wasn't bizarre enough, the lamb was not merely up in the tree, but *upon* the tree. Not caught amongst its branches but growing plum atop, like a sizeable woollen fruit. Edwin stood agog, scratched his head, and tried to convince himself that he must be mistaken by some trick of the light until it happened again. The lamb let out a faint mewling baa. Farmer Tarry stepped forward and took the thin trunk of the tree in one hand. He was not sure what his plan had been, perhaps to shake the strange lamb down, but he had no sooner laid his hand upon it when he jerked it away in surprise. The trunk was warm. Perhaps if it had been a summer's day, and the tree did not stand within the shaded copse, he might not have been so surprised, but as he reached out his hand again, he was alarmed to find something else. Not only was it warm, but it was beating beneath his meaty palm like a steadily thrumming heart. Edwin stood back and stared at it once more, his eyes as round as coins.

Then, he had an idea.

EDWIN RUSHED BACK to the house, his plans dancing merrily in his head. He would cut down the tree and take it to the village. Before the strange wood had withered and died, Edwin could easily charge a small fortune just for folk to look upon the peculiar thing. He could practically hear the rattle of coins in his purse already. He was rummaging in the shed for his axe when Peppin found him. Her round ruddy face was perpetually cross, and her arms were folded at her sturdy aproned waist. Of course, he told her everything. She didn't believe him. She scoffed and laughed and called him a fool. And so, he took her with an axe in hand, to see the strange sight he'd discovered for herself. She spent a few moments considering quietly, her shrewd eyes fixed upon the growing lamb. Her stubby fingers wended their way around the narrow pulsing trunk, and her lips curled.

"We should cut it down," she said.

Cut it down, take it to town and sell it for as much as they could, then be gone from here with what coin they mustered. As Edwin looked at her thin-lipped smile and hungry eyes, he didn't think he had ever loved her so much as this very moment.

PEPPIN WAS BACK at the house, searching for blankets to swaddle the thing in once it had been hacked down. They knew they should keep it covered for the journey—choose the right moment to reveal their prize, lest they attract those that might take it from them. That gave Edwin the task of cutting the strange thing down. He hefted his axe confidently. The trunk was not thick, and he was certain a couple of sharp blows should fell it.

The sun was drooping low when he first struck.

The iron tooth bit deep into the strange tree and sap gushed out like an artery struck. No, not sap. Blood. More blood than Edwin had ever seen come from a thing in his life, and he'd slaughtered more than his share. Above, the strange lamb shrieked as though in pain. It gave Edwin pause, but he gritted his teeth and struck again, biting even deeper this time. A spray of gore covered his forearm, viscous and hot. It had a deep stink, more mould than the metal tang of blood. Disgusted, Farmer Tarry doubled his efforts. By his seventh strike, the stinking blood was all over him, and his arms were growing weak. The sheep still keened above, and the tree still stood proud. In his bitter attacks, Edwin had spread the things bark with his blade and could see something strange.

At the core of the tree, beneath its fleshy bark and thick sinew, was bone. A dense segmented spine that would not chip even with Edwin's meanest strike. Stranger, even as he watched, the gaping wound on the tree began to knit back together.

Exhausted and confused, Edwin dropped to the ground to consider, leaning his back up against the tree. The thing throbbed against his spine. He decided he would fetch his saw and place its jagged edge between the jointed segments; that would surely do his work for him. But when he tried to get back up, something strange happened.

His hand was stuck.

Puzzled, Edwin looked down and what he saw froze his heart like ice.

His hand was gone. In its place, a small mound of thick grass swelled, from which a single daisy sprouted hopefully out. He pulled again, sure that his senses lied—his hand must have slipped beneath a pocket of earth as he sat. As he pulled more fiercely, he saw the blood upon his skin was no longer red, but a dark mossy green. Edwin Tarry opened his mouth to scream, but found it was already full of earth. He tipped back his yawning head, and it stuck to the pulsing tree. He felt it throbbing, more powerful than before, and as he closed his eyes, his own heart began beating to match it.

Peppin Tarry was still awaiting her husband with the ovine fruit of his labour in hand. She shouted for him for a time until she decided the old fool must have gotten distracted and gone to brag to the neighbours about his strange treasure. Peppin marched back to the copse and set her eyes on the tree's crown. What she saw brought a thrill to her heart. There was not just one lamb upon the tree anymore. Beside the first, hanging limp, and only around the size of Peppin's own clenched fist, she could see a second growing.

Peppin spotted her husband's axe on the ground. Hefting it, she scowled at the state in which he kept his tools. It was a rotten thing with its old blade and handle half covered in moss. Dismissing the thought, she rolled up her sleeves then set about her work with a grim smile.

AN OTHER MOUTH TO FEED

Riko Kobayashi had once had the most beautiful hair.

When she'd been small, so many years ago, her mother had brushed it each day at seven o'clock. Over and over until it shone. How little Riko had hated her mother's pretty silver comb. The way it bit her scalp and tugged at her thick black locks brought tears to her eyes. But it wasn't all bad. Sometimes her mother rewarded her with whispers of how the comb's cruel silver teeth looked like stars shooting through her hair, dark and thick as layers of midnight. Each time, when she was finished, her mother would stand her before the large mirror in the hallway and ask her how she looked. Riko would grudgingly admit to her tear-stained reflection that she looked better. She was never allowed to go and play until she had told the little girl standing in the mirror the same thing each time. Your hair looks beautiful.

One day, seven o'clock had arrived, and Riko's mother didn't summon her with the wicked comb in her fingers. Instead, she waited quietly in the sitting room, apparently lost in thought. Riko eventually succumbed and walked to the old mirror and picked up the comb herself. When she presented it to her mother, she'd gifted her the warmest of smiles before she led Riko to the hallway to complete their ritual. After that, Riko never fidgeted or cried while her mother combed her hair again.

Now, Riko was old. Ancient even. She could no longer accurately remember the number of years she'd seen, and if she could, she'd keep that sum secret from all. Her hearing was so dull she could barely hear her own voice, and her eyes clouded until what the mirror showed was mercifully blurred. Her husband—the man whom she had left her country for—was over two decades buried, and she was alone. Alone in the small, tired house they'd shared for so many years. Many of the bulbs were too fiddly for her gnarled hands to replace alone and instead gathered dust in the dimness; a faded memory of the times she'd tended her own daughter's hair in this house with her mother's silver comb. Now that child, Mae, lived far away, surrounded by her own children and grandchildren to rear, and a full life to lead.

The gnawing ache in Riko's hip rose as she walked carefully down the hallway where the dull yellow glow of the last living lamp warmed the deep red walls. She stopped, as she did each night in front of the mirror, to pick up the silver comb on its ledge. As she did, she caught sight of the old woman that lived in the mirror now. Her face was unfamiliar. Creased deeply from years of laughter and framed by the thick white layers of hair dry and pale as bone that hung almost to the floor. She took up the comb in her stiff fingers and closed her eyes as she completed the first stroke.

~

"Hurry up," the man growled, his breath steaming in the cool night. He pushed his hands deeper into the pockets of his parka and glanced either way down the street from beneath his grubby baseball cap. Seven o'clock was far too early to be pulling this kind of shit, no matter if everyone that lived on this block was pushing a hundred and winter meant it was already full dark.

Chitty Osborne was not evil per se, but he was more than familiar with the darkness that lived inside him. It had been there for as long as he could remember—even before he'd taken up his more unsavoury pursuits. It coiled inside his chest, waiting for something to make him slip, to loosen his grip so that it could take control. His Ma hadn't known the half of it when she told him he had the devil inside him.

"I said hurry!" He delivered a short sharp kick to the boots of the man hunched beside him.

Well, 'man' might have been generous.

The kid didn't answer, but Chitty caught the curl of his lip from below his deep hood as he continued to jimmy the lock.

Eddie was gonna hear about this alright. This jumped-up little shit had sworn these old houses were easy pickings, with locks fit to drop out of the wood that held them. The kid claimed he'd been stealing from the old folks around here for months. Same time as he took half of them their meals on wheels, he took a little something himself in return. A ring, some banknotes out of a purse, and one time a heap of fancy-looking silverware that turned out to be worth shit. Only he'd lifted nothing from *this* house because he'd never been inside. The kid claimed neither he nor the neighbours saw anyone come in or out of this house in months. Chitty figured whatever coffin dodger lived here was in a home or visiting family elsewhere. Worst case, they'd find a bloated body half-eaten by a hungry pack of friendly cats.

A car rumbled past the end of the street, lights flashing dangerously close to their location, and for a second Chitty thought it might turn in. The darkness in his chest shuddered to wakefulness, hungry for trouble.

The car passed by.

"Kid," he warned, that keen edge entering his voice.

The kid mumbled something in reply as his fingers worked.

There was a click, and the little shit shot him a look that was equal parts relieved and triumphant.

"Yeah, yeah," Chitty snarled.

The kid hopped up, tucking his pick in his pocket, and moved to turn the handle.

Chitty grabbed his wrist roughly. "When you can grow a beard, then you get to go in first."

The kid looked hurt and rubbed the patchy growth on his chin.

Chitty chuckled, pushed the door open, and strode in.

He damned near shit himself when he saw the old Asian woman standing there.

She was barely as tall as his chest and looked older than anyone he'd ever seen, her face sagging despite the shock in her eyes. Her long white hair fanned over her shoulders like a sheet, and her frail hands clutched to the chest of her ridiculous frilly nightgown.

If the shock of seeing her was a wound, the darkness inside him welled from it like vital blood. It expanded inside his chest, filling all the empty spaces he had.

The kid bumped into the back of him.

"Fuck, shut the door!" Chitty spat as he snatched his knife out of his pocket. It wasn't much of a knife, but it had a point, and an edge sharp enough to end a life.

The old woman gave out a strangled scream when he flicked it open.

"Quiet lady, we just want your stuff, we don't want to hurt you."

The beast in his chest screamed he was a liar; begged her to give him some excuse. He'd never hurt an old lady before.

"You understand English?" Chitty asked.

The old woman whimpered, clutching her fists tighter to her chest.

The kid's voice came shakily from behind him. "Maybe we should just—"

"Shut the fuck up!" Chitty's eyes never left the old woman. He let a rictus smile split his face. "Listen, you old bitch, I won't ask again. Do you speak fucking English?"

The old woman gave a shaking nod, a single fat tear rolling slowly down her wrinkled cheek.

"Where's your jewellery? Money?" He enunciated each word loud and slow. The darkness pounded in his chest, begging to be released, pumping into his veins, tightening his grip on his knife. Making him stronger.

The old woman nodded toward the door beside where Chitty stood and tried to speak, but only a feeble whimper escaped.

Chitty forced that wild grin onto his face harder, knowing he looked practically demonic. "Now, don't you fucking move. Don't make a sound, or you'll be sorry."

Another tear rolled down the old woman's cheek.

"Don't let her out of your sight," Chitty said.

The kid stumbled forward, trying to look menacing, but his long limbs and wide eyes spoiled the effect, making him look more like an angry puppet.

The room the woman had directed him to was small and tidy. A sizeable ornate dresser stood in front of him, and a small sofa beside a TV that looked like it probably didn't even run colour. He un-shouldered his backpack as he made a beeline for the dresser, yanking out the closest drawer, which was full of worthless knickknacks and old papers. He shoved it back in and started rifling through the others.

"Um...she has something." The kid's still shaking voice echoed from the hallway.

"What?" Chitty slammed another drawer shut. Fucking napkins.

"It's shiny. Some kind of comb?"

Chitty shook his head angrily as he rummaged through a cabinet. "Then fucking take it from her, you little asshole."

Three more drawers and a cupboard gave him some old useless letters, some cutlery that looked silver, and rings for the fucking napkins that looked like they might be, too. But nothing else. No money, no jewellery.

The darkness in his chest howled.

"Ask her where the fuck the good stuff is." Chitty slammed the last drawer closed.

Silence.

"Kid?" Chitty yelled.

There was a thump.

Chitty shouldered his bag angrily and strode to the doorway.

The darkness raged in his chest.

"Kid, I told you to ask her—"

His muscles froze.

The old woman stood where she had before, her dark eyes fixed on him sharply.

The kid was behind her, doing something weird.

Chitty took another step and tripped. No, something snatched his leg, and an arm snaked around his neck, squeezing his throat. He lashed out with his meagre blade.

The thing in his chest rejoiced as he set it free.

But his arm only connected clumsily with the wall beside him, missing whoever had apprehended him completely. Confused, Chitty tried to yell out, but whoever had hold of him forced something into his mouth, something soft that muffled his cry. Chitty's eyes searched for his attacker. It wasn't a person. It was...hair?

There was a thud, and he saw that the kid had fallen to

the floor, only not all of him. His neck ended at a mangled ruin where his head used to be. Acid burned at Chitty's throat, and he retched, but the hair only pushed deeper into his mouth, filling his gullet. He felt it squeezing tighter around his waist.

Something pulled him.

The hair pulled him.

His feet left the floor with the strength of it as he watched in disbelief as more of those snowy locks writhed around the woman in the dull light.

She shook her head gently as her hair dragged him closer.

His toes scraped along the floor, muffled shouts wracking his body.

She tutted gently, as though scolding a wayward child.

Now he was close, he could see her better. Why had he ever thought she was old? There were only fine lines at the corners of her eyes, and her hair was not white, but a dull metallic grey.

The woman shifted something carefully in her hands.

Through his tear-streaked eyes, he saw it was indeed a beautiful silver comb.

"I did not plan to do this again," the woman purred softly, amused. Her accented voice was thick and smooth, like honey. "But fate has a way of stepping in sometimes." She smirked, turning to give him her back.

The hair pulled again, dragging him closer.

Chitty's eyes bulged. The back of her head was...not there. Instead, it opened into a full crimson smile, rows of jagged teeth covered in blood and gore. Parts of the kid, he realised numbly.

Whatever darkness had ever lived within him fled all at once. The beast that had coiled within his chest for as long as he could remember evaporated. His body suddenly felt weak, limbs hanging limp in the seemingly endless hair around him. Tears blurred his vision.

The thing that lived inside him was nothing compared to this. *This* was a real monster.

The hair pulled him in inexorably, crushing around his throat and waist until he thought he was going to pass out—he *wished* he would. He pleaded for the mercy of consciousness abandoning him. Instead, he felt the heat of fetid breath on his face and a burning pressure as the mouth closed around his head. Sharp, searing, agonising pain. Hot, slick wet running down his neck. The crunch of teeth on bone.

Riko Kobayashi checked the door was closed, carefully propping an ornate chair from the dining table under the handle. She would need to get a locksmith to come and fix that tomorrow. Well, when she'd tidied up the mess—not that there was much left now.

Stepping over what remained of the younger one, she stood before the mirror, and a surprised gasp escaped her.

She'd almost forgotten what she looked like.

Filled with wonder, she carefully lifted her silver comb and began to brush.

She'd been alive for around for several of what most people would call lifetimes. She'd borne seventeen children, four of whom carried the gene—two that still lived. This time, she'd thought, would really be it for her. Her end. When Harold had passed, she'd decided not to feed again. Her life had been long, and she'd taken what joy she could find. She'd learned to ignore the hunger for so long that it was barely there anymore, just a dull ache deep in her core. But now...

Her skin was smooth and supple, her once rheumy eyes

sharp and clear, and her hair! It was thick and lustrous, like molten night flowing from her crown. Her mind rushed with possibilities. Perhaps they would tell people she was one of her granddaughters' friends? A relative from Japan? She could move in with them, look after her own great-grandchildren as a nanny. She'd not had a female lover for so long, perhaps this time—

Her mother's silver comb snagged, and something fell to the floor. Her eyes followed it, bemused.

A human tooth.

Riko brushed it aside with her foot, and it skittered across the floorboards and came to rest against the older one's remains. She caught sight of the state of the shining comb in her hand, streaked with dark congealing blood. Tutting, she set it down carefully. Riko paused and checked her reflection once more, drinking in the sight of herself. Then, she said words to herself that she had not spoken for many years.

"Your hair looks beautiful."

4

NO PLACE LIKE HOME
PART TWO

After his confrontation with Knud, Daniel ran straight to his bedroom and threw himself beneath the covers. He huddled there as though he were seven years old again and had suffered a particularly horrible nightmare, and the blankets were all the armour he needed from the threats outside. The blankets, however, didn't blind his mind's eye from the memory of those red eyes and pointed teeth. Daniel was just considering what would happen if he called the police when that sound started again. The low rumbling moan.

It sounded like...crying.

Daniel listened for what might have been hours, barely even daring to breathe under his sheets. He wasn't sure what happened first—either the crying stopped, or he fell into an exhausted sleep—but when Daniel awoke, the haunting sobs had gone, and there was only the soft sound of birdsong through the window. Part of him wanted to believe it had all been a dream, but he knew in his bones that Knud was as real as the manor itself.

Had that *thing* really lived here all this time? Aunt Bea

must've known, of course, but what had Knud been to her? She'd been the one to tell Daniel never to visit the cottage. The one always sitting at the kitchen table smiling beside the freshly baked goods in the morning, smiling like she'd just been talking with an old friend.

These thoughts galloped around Daniel's mind as he cautiously made his way downstairs, rumpled and tired in his pyjamas. There was a familiar smell drifting from the kitchen. When he entered, Daniel was once again almost surprised not to find Aunt Bea waiting. Instead, was a pie. Apricot, Daniel knew by the smell—his favourite. But there was something strange about the top of it. Rough letters shaped from excess pastry atop the golden baked fruit. Daniel imagined such a delicate task might be tricky for fingers like Knud's. A bakery might've hesitated to call it rustic. It was only one word.

Sorry.

~

THREE DAYS PASSED.

Daniel might've been able to convince himself Knud wasn't real if not for his clothes seeming to launder and fold themselves and the delicious food that kept appearing on the table. He was sitting in the leather captain's chair in the office, staring at the space where he'd seen Knud, when the doorbell rang.

It was a sound he hadn't heard for so long that it didn't register at first.

He made his way to the door, glimpsing himself in the hallway mirror as he passed. Daniel swept a wave of his reddish hair back behind his ear and straightened his glasses, noting that he needed to shave later.

The doorbell rang again, a tinkling chime that pulled him back to his purpose.

Perhaps it was the local grocer.

Daniel wondered if it was still Mr Simpkins, though he'd surely retired by now. No doubt they'd heard about Aunt Bea's passing, but with Daniel back, they'd probably keep arrangements as they were—at least until he figured out what he'd do with the manor.

What he'd do about Knud.

When Daniel opened the door, however, he did not find Mr Simpkins or any other grocer. Instead, he almost swallowed his tongue.

His parents stood upon the steps.

His mother wore a charcoal blazer bedazzled with gaudy brooches and an ankle-length skirt. Her crisp, white blouse made her coral lipstick pop—she'd applied extra of that, perhaps to fill the crow's feet around her lips. She tilted her head back, looking down her nose regally with the same hazel eyes as his. Her blonde hair didn't show a hint of grey, a precise marvel of maintenance in a sensible bun. His father looked tired. His neatly trimmed moustache was as white as the last wisps of hair on his head, and his gold-rimmed glasses were slightly foggy. Daniel had always thought he looked like a teacher, but his tweed patched suit announced it proudly.

"Daniel." His mother's eyes creased in what might be a smile that didn't quite find her mouth. "Wouldn't you like to invite us in?"

Daniel's mouth flapped like a fish out of water, flabbergasted.

His mother snatched the initiative and marched straight through the doorway, forcing him to step aside, her kitten heels punishing the flagstones.

Daniel's father's eyes were elusive as he followed.

"Tea?" his mother asked, clutching her powder blue handbag to her chest daintily.

It took Daniel a second to realise it was more a demand than an offer. "Uh...yes. Alright."

"We'll take it in the conservatory," she announced, already heading that way with a clicking of heels.

A clicking Daniel thought eerily akin to the sound of cloven hooves.

Daniel was just trying to remember which cupboard Aunt Bea kept the tea in when he spotted a steaming pot already brewing on the worktop. A small silver dish of sugar and an adorably gaudy cow shaped jug with most of the paintwork worn off filled with milk sat beside it.

Knud.

Daniel's eyes hunted, scanning the back door and by the pantry. How did something so big have such a knack for creeping around?

And what would his parents do if Knud popped out?

Almost smiling at that thought, Daniel picked up the tray and carried it back to the conservatory.

THE ONLY SOUND in the conservatory was the slurping of his father sucking tea through his moustache.

His mother fixed him with that peculiar gaze again, as if trying to pin him down with her eyes to examine him, staring at something she didn't want to see but needed to understand.

Daniel shifted uncomfortably in his seat. Why did he feel fifteen again? Why had he even invited them in?

Well, he hadn't actually invited them in at all, had he.

"Quite fortuitous, with everything at the reading." His mother's eyes crinkled once more, but her mouth remained compressed in a straight line. "I hear you've been doing well in New York?"

Daniel reeled. "What?"

She waved her hand as if shooing away his nonsense. "Oh, Daniel. As if we wouldn't get every update we could from your dear Aunt Beatrice. You're our son, after all. Just because we couldn't offer you the upbringing you deserved does not mean that we don't love you."

His father slurped noisily again, his eyes fixed straight ahead.

Daniel's breath was suddenly very tight in his chest.

"My love," his mother cooed. "Your father and I were horribly poor whilst you were a child. When your uncle died, Aunt Beatrice was lonely out here. We simply saw the opportunity to offer you a better life and ensure she wasn't living in solitude."

Daniel frowned, the words catching in too many places at once in his head to pick apart thoroughly. Strangely, it was the last that rang most false of all. She *hadn't* been out here all alone, had she.

Daniel cleared his throat. "You left me here. I wrote letters, but you never responded. You never called or visited."

"Oh, sweet boy, we didn't want to make you homesick. We knew you'd have a better life here, and indeed, look at you: thriving!" His mother gestured around them grandly, waggling teacup and spilling some of it's contents on the tabletop.

Daniel took a slow breath. "So, it wasn't because I'm gay."

His father choked on a mouthful of tea and his mother looked like she'd just swallowed a bee.

"Darling," she spluttered. "As long as you are happy, that's what counts. We would never deny you joy."

Daniel grunted, folding his arms. The shock was settling somewhat now, but he could feel the strings being attached to his limbs by his mother's words. He remembered the tone and cadence of her words well; they were how she had spoken to his aunt and uncle when he was a boy. Daniel knew exactly what she was going to say next.

"Just as I know that you'd never deny ours." She sighed dramatically for effect, her mouth downturned to an almost pantomime like degree. "You see, since we allowed you to be with Aunt Beatrice, our own lives became quite difficult. Your father lost tenure—politics at the University—and you know I've always had my hands too full with running the house to take on extra work."

Daniel resisted the temptation to laugh. As he recalled it, she'd barely lifted a finger around the house.

His mother batted her spidery lashes. "You see, we were rather counting on a gesture of kindness promised by your dear Aunt Beatrice. After all these years, and us sharing the love of our only child with her to enrich her life, she was to share some of her own blessings with us. But alas, it seems as if there has been some slight mistake."

Daniel's father's eyes finally met his, if only for a moment. Grey-blue and steely. His gaze was penetrating and keen, but also uncomfortable, and darted away like he'd been jolted with a bolt of electricity.

"Mistake?" Daniel ventured blandly.

"Yes, dear. Aunt Beatrice promised us the accounts and planned to leave the manor for you—she'd always wanted it to be so—but in the last few years, with you being so successful in America, she was amidst the process of changing the will so you'd get the accounts instead. She thought the money would serve you best, and this dusty old manor would be an excellent consolation for your father and I."

Suddenly, there was a loud, snapping noise, and her chair collapsed beneath her. She let out a screech, her arms flinging up in the air as she tumbled from view, her teacup clattering onto the table.

Daniel's father rushed to hoist her up with both hands under her armpits. Strands of her platinum hair had flown awry in the fall, and though flustered, she looked otherwise intact.

Daniel struggled not to laugh and cleared his throat instead.

"You see, darling?" His mother was not to be deterred as she dusted herself off. The contents of her cup had emptied over her pristine blouse in a stain that would surely never leave. "This place is falling apart!"

The floorboards upstairs creaked loudly, and his parents looked up at the ceiling above, confused.

"Do you have people here?" his mother asked weakly. "A gentleman caller, perhaps?"

Daniel shook his head but didn't miss the sneer on his father's face.

"No, just me," Daniel lied.

The creaking upstairs and the breaking chair; Daniel suspected Knud somehow had something to do with both.

His mother sighed. "Well, my love, as I was saying, your aunt wanted to give us this run-down old place—"

The floorboards moaned again. Louder this time. Not only that, but the doors whined on their hinges and the windows rattled in their frames.

His mother fell silent, staring around, aghast.

Daniel jumped at the opportunity.

"You know what? I think I've had enough visitors for the day. Jonathan, Karen, I think you should leave."

His mother's mouth flapped, but his father's face darkened.

"How dare you speak to your mother that way!" he snarled, raising a finger.

Ah yes, the waggling finger. Daniel wondered if he should feel intimidated. This man featured in the nightmares of countless children over the years, indeed, he'd been a staple in Daniel's own. But were those empty words really the best he could do after this long?

The smile Daniel allowed to form on his lips came easily. "I dare. Now get out."

His father's face purpled, his lips twisting in contempt.

"Now, now, Jonathan. Daniel has had an arduous week, let's talk about this another time." The performative pleasantness of his mother's voice sounded strained.

The house groaned.

"How about let's not?" Daniel said darkly. "How about you get out of my house, with neither the manor nor the accounts. And then, I suggest you never talk to me again."

His mother's eyes bulged.

"You listen here, boy," his father spat.

The house groaned again. No, it *wailed*. Daniel could feel the floorboards shaking under his feet. At its peak, one more sound joined it, a low and rumbling growl like a lion's dangerous purr.

Daniel knew Knud was close.

All the blood that had filled his father's face rushed out, and his mother practically wilted. All at once, the moaning rattle stopped, and the entire house fell into a deathly silence.

Daniel spoke softly but firmly. "Get. Out."

His parents fled to the door, and his father flung it open. Neither looked back, but his mother was not entirely out before it slammed shut on her backside of its own accord, ejecting her with a shriek.

To be continued...

5

THE WORST SPICE

"Jesus, Arthur! You need to get that looked at." Ella sighed. This must have been the hundredth time they'd said it.

Arthur shrugged, flashing them a rictus, yellowed smile. His gums were so receded that it couldn't be much longer until his skull showed when he grinned like that. His voice was even raspier than usual. "When you get to my age, you don't have to do as you're told."

Ella grunted, setting the bag of food down on the countertop. "Maybe, but if you don't get it seen, you might not live much longer to keep ignoring me."

Arthur's ginger cat, Brando, stalked over curiously, poking his nose into the top of the bag to inspect its contents.

"I think I preferred it when you called me Mr Williams." Arthur's jowls wobbled in disdain. He pulled the threadbare fleece throw tighter around his shoulders, covering the suspicious lump at the base of his neck from further scrutiny.

The hideous blanket—a sickly shade of pea green—was ill-suited to the task. The bump had ballooned over the last couple of weeks and was now the size of an egg. Arthur might have been pushing a hundred, so he surely knew that was bad. Seeing such rapid growth gave Ella a sick feeling in their stomach. They knew what that meant. Uncle Gary had a lump on his wrist a little smaller than that. It wasn't long until it was red and angry, and a few weeks later he'd been dead. Rhabdomyosarcoma. Ella had dropped out of nursing school because they couldn't handle the pressure, but they'd always had a head for the names of conditions. Their interest in that —and the simple pleasure they took in helping people—meant their current job delivering food to the elderly was a natural fit.

"Ain't you supposed to just bring me my dinner and piss off? I din't think they paid you to be giving me advice," Arthur grumbled.

Ella forced a grin and offered Arthur a wink. "It can't be Mr Williams when you're in a bad mood and Arthur when you're happy. And I don't go around giving advice to everyone, only for the people I like."

"Well, if you like me so much, why don't you bring me better portions?" Arthur's eyes glittered with mischief, but the scowl never left his wizened face.

He'd had almost a century to practice those scowls.

One day Ella hoped to perfect that disapproving glare to even a shadow of Arthur's masterpiece.

"I already give you double! They only put a couple of spares in the van, and I give you whatever I can."

Arthur let out a loud harrumph, folding his thin arms sulkily.

Reaching out to rub Brando behind one velvety ear on the counter, Ella eyed the old man curiously. Beneath the ugly blanket and loose pyjamas, Arthur was notably scrawny. The skin on his elbows and hands was like tracing paper, showing the dark veins beneath. "Are you sharing your meals, Arthur?

You know, if you tell me, I could probably work something out."

"I'm not!" the old man barked. The effort shook his blanket loose again, revealing the bulging mass beneath.

Ella's eyes drifted back toward it unerringly. It looked awful. Swollen and hard, and...was it pulsating? That meant it had vascularity, right? That was a bad thing. It could be a sign of a nasty tumour.

"Are you really so starved for attention that you're eyeing up a codger like me?" Arthur asked slyly, then chuckled wetly at the face Ella pulled. "I told you, you spend too much time around old folks—you should get out more. When I was your age, I was polishing more knobs than a housekeeper in a hotel."

This was fairly mild for Arthur, but Ella's cheeks still flooded with colour.

Rainbow Wheels was a food delivery and elderly companion program for LGBTQIA+ pensioners, so there was no shortage of colourful characters on the books. Just before getting here, Ella had spent an hour with Brian, who'd been a drag performer for decades. Brian was showing signs of dementia that meant his old drag persona could take over at any given moment. He'd whip out the nearest matted wig from who knows where and launch into a show tune at the strangest times. Arthur here wasn't the most fabulous personality on the roster, but he'd always been Ella's favourite. There was a deep sadness about him that just resonated with them. However, whenever they tried to bring up Arthur's past, the old man was more slippery than an eel.

"Hold up," Arthur said suddenly, sitting bolt upright. "A couple?"

Ella looked up at him, confused. "What?"

"You said they give you a couple of spares. You give me

double, so that means you have one more in the van." The old man's eyes were sharp and flinty.

"I do," Ella admitted. The portion they usually ate themself for lunch, parked up on the hills near to here. Both the pay and food from Rainbow Wheels was mediocre, so Marion, the manager, at least kept the drivers fed.

"Then why don't you let me have it?" Arthur asked, his voice suddenly sweet.

A thought occurred to Ella, and they suppressed a grin. This could work to their advantage. "Okay, but on one condition."

Arthur's eyes narrowed.

"Call the Doctor and get that lump checked out."

A WEEK LATER, Ella arrived outside Arthur's flat again, this time with triple the standard meals in two large paper bags. They tapped gently on the door. After a few minutes with no answer, they popped out the spare key Arthur had given Rainbow Wheels and opened the door.

Ella knew Arthur was dead the second the smell hit them.

The sweet, sickly stink of decay and excrement.

It wasn't uncommon to find a body in this line of work—three in just the last year, in fact—but never one with a stink this bad.

Ella's heart sank with guilt. They liked Arthur and didn't want this stench to be their last memory of the grumpy old bastard.

Steeling themself, Ella let the door close behind them. Taking slow, shallow breaths through their mouth, they made their way over to the counter. Wherever the body was, it couldn't be far. Christ, how had it gotten this bad? Andy, the weekend delivery driver, would have visited on Saturday. It was only Tuesday now, so just what kind of—

"You brought it all?" Arthur's voice was sharp and brittle.

Ella jolted in surprise. "Jesus Arthur, I—" They spun around, and found the old man standing in the doorway of the connecting bedroom. "Shit, you look awful."

The old man didn't even flinch. Delicate wisps of wiry white hair stood up at odd angles from his head. He was shrouded in that hideous green blanket again and his eyes shone with feverish intensity. His reedy voice was little more than a snarl. "You brought the extra food?"

"Are you alright, Arthur?" Ella set the bags down on the counter. Their eyes scanned the old man. Was he still wearing the same pyjamas as last week?

Arthur's thin lips pressed tightly together. "The food," he growled again.

"Uh, yeah. It's all here." Ella gestured to the bags, then noticed something strange. The usual visitor was not inspecting their offering. "Where's Brando?"

"Gone!" Arthur barked.

Ella shot him a look of confusion. "What's going on, Arthur?"

The old man pulled the blanket tighter around himself, glowering as he waddled over.

Ella struggled not to recoil as he brought his stink closer. As politely as possible, they vacated the space between Arthur and the food on the counter.

As Arthur shuffled past, Ella caught sight of dark stains on his pyjamas. Their heart sank and bile rose in their throat.

Arthur snatched up one bag, pulling out a container, and as he did, his blanket slipped loose.

Ella was already pulling out their phone to call for help when they saw it.

The lump on Arthur's neck was even more prominent

now—huge in fact. Less like an egg and more like a ripe peach. Where his skin hung slack everywhere else, it pulled taut over the swollen, throbbing mass. He was unfastening the lid of the Tupperware. Ella watched, nauseated, as the old man's filthy fingers pushed into the rice and shovelled it into his dribbling mouth.

Gagging, Ella twisted and let themself out of the front door. The latch clicked shut behind them before they doubled over and heaved.

After a few moments of managing not to actually vomit, Ella tried to gather their thoughts. The old man was usually sharp and acerbic, and a little prickly about his hygiene. Something was definitely very wrong. Pulling their phone out, Ella called Marion.

"Hey," Marion answered lazily. "What's up?"

Ella's voice shook. "I'm at Arthur Williams'. He's a total mess, covered in...he's soiled himself, I think. He's just not right. I think he's sick. He's got this lump on his neck. I don't know if he's septic or what."

Marion hummed thoughtfully down the line. "I should have checked on him. Andy didn't finish his rounds on Saturday. Left the van by Brian's and buggered off. He must've seen the state of Arthur and panicked, he's not answered his phone all weekend."

"What should I do?"

"Get him sitting down, keep him calm, and call an ambulance," Marion said. "Call me when you're done and let me know how it went."

Ella swallowed. "Okay, I'll try."

Ella thought they were prepared to return to the stink, but it was even worse when they opened the door again.

Arthur had his back to them at the countertop, hunched over, still shovelling food greedily into his mouth.

Ella steeled themself but didn't take a deep breath to do it. "Okay, Arthur, I'm back. Why don't you come and have a seat and we can talk?"

Arthur ignored them, smacking his lips wetly instead.

Ella took another step closer.

Slowly the old man straightened, the blanket slipping away completely.

Ella huffed a breath out, wincing, and trying to focus their eyes on the back of the old man's head instead of his soiled pyjamas. Their eyes slid down the old man's silver crown to search for the growth on his neck, but...

Ella leaned forward.

What? That's impossible.

The lump was gone.

Was it the angle? No. That thing had been big enough that you could have seen it through the window from across the street. Maybe it had been some kind of cyst that had just burst?

The old man turned, holding a fist full of wet stewed meat in one filthy hand before his face, his eyes fixed and glassy, pupils dilated in bliss. But his mouth...

Arthur's mouth was forced impossibly wide, like his jaw had been unhinged. Between his thin lips, something like a fat white slug hung out, only it was like no slug Ella had ever seen. It was far too big for a slug and it had small jagged teeth in a sore looking puckered mouth about as big as a pound coin. Little tentacles, like those belonging to a tiny fleshy octopus, squirmed out either side of the old man's gaping mouth like worms.

Ella stared in horror.

The food carton hit the ground, scattering rice and stew

all over their feet. They hadn't even seen it slip from the old man's fingers.

Ella's breath escaped them in a shuddering moan. "Arthur...I...I think we should..."

The old man took a slow step toward them. The pale squid-slug-thing in his mouth squirmed, its small jaws flapping open hungrily.

Panic took the wheel firmly away from horror, and reason was a distant speck in the rear-view mirror as Ella turned toward the door and bolted.

At least that's what they tried to do.

In their haste, Ella's feet caught on one another, and they stumbled awkwardly. The slick stew spattered on the tiled floor squeaked as it foiled their attempt, and instead pitched them forward, phone pirouetting out of their hand and through the air. Ella's chest collided with the floor with enough force to knock the wind out of them with a wheezing thud. Their fingers desperately clawed the floor, trying to pull themself to their feet.

There was a strange bubbling growl from behind them.

Ella let out a fearful cry, scrambling on their hands and knees to get away from Arthur—away from whatever the hideous thing living inside him was.

Staggering to their feet, Ella darted for the door, but in their dazed haste, found themself at the bedroom door instead. They turned around to get out of the flat, but... Arthur.

A strange wormy tendril wriggled its way back between Arthur's lips like a dreadful noodle. "Don't go," he rasped. "I'm hungry."

Ella's mouth flapped wordlessly.

With a disturbing, lurching speed, the old man moved toward them.

"Stop it, Arthur. Stay back!" Ella wailed, stumbling back

into the bedroom, raising their hands. Something caught the back of their feet, and they tumbled, landing with a heavy thud, head bouncing off the floor. Their ears rang with the force of it. Stunned and blinking, they looked to the side.

The old man's bed was beside them, bundled clothes beneath.

No. Not clothes. Legs.

Ella's eyes travelled numbly up the legs to find dark drying blood crusting the ugly old beige carpet. A pale arm stuck out from beneath the bed. Ella stared at the empty eye sockets like yawning bloody caverns in the slack, pale face, mouth wide in a last scream.

Andy.

No wonder he didn't finish his rounds. His throat was a torn flap of flesh, cords, and sinew.

The sound of stumbling steps coming toward them jolted Ella out of their hypnotic state, and they struggled to their knees.

The old man was coming. Too close for Ella to get out of the door. Instead, they slammed it shut. Arthur collided with it with rattling force, and one of the panels splintered. Ella let out a shrill cry, and threw their body forward to reinforce it.

How was he so strong?

Ella's eyes searched the door desperately for a lock. Then around the room for a wedge of some kind that they could use to hold the door in place, but failed.

Panting, they waited.

Silence.

No twisting of the knob.

Nothing.

Maybe...Maybe the old man had done himself in. The force he'd hit the door with had almost been enough to tear it off its hinges. He was probably lying on the floor outside, bleeding from the head, wheezing his final breaths.

Ella panted.

Good. Let him be dead. Please, God, let him be dead.

Ella carefully edged their back away from the door, sweat soaking their T-shirt, sticking it to their skin. Careful not to make too much sound, they climbed to their knees. They stared at the handle for an entire minute, expecting it to twist, ready to snatch it and hold it still.

But it didn't.

Ella took a long breath out and got to their feet.

Then there was an almighty crash against the door, a splintering crunch as the hinges tore loose. Ella wasn't fast enough to get their hands up in time as it tumbled toward their head.

ELLA BLINKED. Their vision was blurry. They raised a hand to their forehead, before snatching it back with a hiss from the sharp sticky throb. Blood on their fingertips. Not much, but not good.

Groggily, they tried to move, but found their body trapped. Looking down, Ella saw the broken door was half on top of them, pinning them down.

That was when they remembered Arthur and whatever that thing was that had been inside him.

Terror energised Ella's body with a spasm. They pushed at the door, flinging it off, sending its broken remains to tilt against the bed. Andy's pale arm peeked out from under it. Now Ella could see meaty chunks were missing from that, too. They wanted to vomit and weren't sure if it was the head injury or just everything else.

Groaning, they sat up.

Arthur lay crumpled nearby.

His limbs were splayed at awkward angles, his left

shoulder thrown back, dislocated from being used as a battering ram to break down the door. His eyes stared unseeing and his mouth was slack and open. A trail of dark blood ran from his lips.

Dead.

Thank God.

Groaning in pain, Ella struggled to their feet.

Beyond Arthur, they could see their phone on the floor.

Ella carefully stepped over the old man's body, picking up the phone and clutching it in their shaking hands.

It was time to call for help, but what was the right thing to say? No one would believe what just happened.

They swayed on their feet, dizzily.

Maybe best to take a minute first.

Ella's stomach rumbled, and their eyes fell on the bag of meals left on the countertop. A deep, ravenous hunger hummed inside them.

Well, it wouldn't hurt. The old man was already dead, no matter how quick the ambulance got here.

Ella's appetite took over, and they hungrily pulled the food out of the bag and set it on the table, then popped open a drawer and took a spoon. Ella cast an apologetic glance at Arthur's body. "Sorry, buddy. Figured you wouldn't mind sharing, though. You owe me one." They rubbed the back of their aching head tenderly. As their hand moved away, it caught against something on the side of their throat. Something that hadn't been there before.

Ella froze, and a shudder ran through their body. Ever so slowly, they moved their shaking fingers, and gingerly traced the lump on their neck.

6

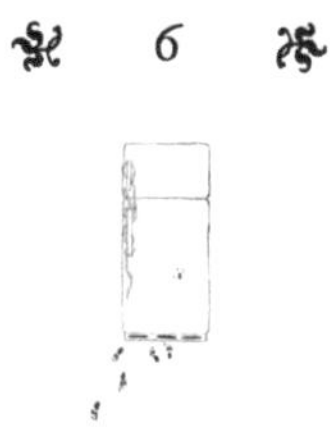

A MIDNIGHT SNACK

Ryan yawned and rubbed his eyes.

Just another terrible night's sleep.

His phone buzzed on the nightstand. He picked it up, smirking as the nickname he'd given his mother in his phonebook appeared. At least that was always good for a laugh.

HOW R U?

MOTHRA

I'm okay, Mom. Just tired. Still having trouble sleeping.

RYAN

Granted, he *had* been up until past three with the glowing light of his laptop burning into his retinas, but it was almost noon. Ever since he'd been left to his own devices, he'd drifted back into the sleeping realm of a brooding adolescent. His thirty-something-year-old body certainly had something to say about that. Brandon had always been a stickler for a clean sleep routine.

Does that mean I'm a dirty sleeper now?

Ryan untangled himself from his bedclothes, standing and stretching with another yawn. In boxers and T-shirt, he lumbered from the bedroom and into the kitchen. He set his phone on the countertop and flicked the switch to get the stainless-steel coffee god humming, then, he almost slipped and fell flat on his ass in the cold puddle by the fridge.

"Fuck, shit, what?" He blinked at the pool on the dark wooden floor. Was that...milk?

His phone buzzed on the counter.

Hopping over, leaving droplets of milk in his wake, Ryan grabbed the roll of kitchen towel and yanked off several squares, tossing them on top of the pool of milk. Brandon would have hated that. He seemed to think that if you used one square first, you wouldn't end up using the other five after a big spill. That wasn't why they'd broken up, of course.

Jesus, maybe it was.

It was all the little bullshit things like who washed the dishes or which way the toilet roll hung that went from being laughable to mind-bending in a series of years. He yanked loose three more squares just to spite his ex and pressed them down with his bare foot. He out down the kitchen roll and checked his phone.

IT'S THIS QUARANTINE. YOU HAVE TOO MUCH STRESS. HAVE YOU TALKED TO DR WALTERS?

MOTHRA

Isolation Mom, not quarantine. Quarantine is if you actually have the virus. And no, I'm fine.

RYAN

Ryan set the phone back down, perhaps a little harder than necessary. He didn't want to talk to Doctor Walters.

Mainly because he knew sleep disruption meant he wasn't doing well, but also it seemed he had a new symptom, too. Just when he'd finally found the balance in meds that had been keeping him levelled out most of the day without making him feel like he was living in third person. Gritting his teeth, he opened the fridge door to assess the damage. This had been going on a few weeks now. His sleep was restless, he woke up in panics in the night, and every other day the fridge was left open in the morning. Leftovers had been dropped on the floor, and a big bite taken out of his best cheese. Apparently, sleep eating was a thing, and a thing he now did. He hissed when he saw the state of the inside of the fridge today. A carton of milk was tipped over and a fistful of left-over pasta he'd made for lunch yesterday was snatched out of the bowl. He checked his fingers.

Huh. Is sleep hand washing a thing, too?

Frowning, he went back to his damage report.

Some things were entirely missing.

His shopping had only been delivered yesterday. He'd ordered bacon and sausages, and a couple of good steaks, but now they were nowhere to be seen. In fact, all the meat had gone.

Ryan looked around the living area but came up empty handed. "Fuck!"

Brandon had been kind of a neat freak, and the apartment had a whole minimalist loft vibe. Optimal for work, he'd claimed—like he was the one that worked from home and not Ryan. Even with Brandon months gone, nothing had changed. The benefit of the sleek styling was that there wasn't anywhere to hide stuff. There was no sign of any rogue fridge contents strewn around.

A thought occurred to Ryan, and his skin prickled.

Slamming the messy fridge shut, Ryan marched to the front door. His eyes travelled quickly over the deadbolts and latches. All in order. His heart pounded in his chest. For a moment, he'd almost thought someone had been sneaking in to steal his food—fuck knows what'd happened to it, though. Maybe he'd thrown it out the window. He didn't exactly plan to go outside and check. There was another dull *bzzt* from his phone on the countertop. Ryan made his way back, deciding he'd at least have some toast before he sorted out the mess in the fridge.

RYAN AWOKE WITH A START.

He stared at the ceiling. The pale light of the moon spilled through the thin gap in the curtains. For a moment, he lay on the precipice between sleep and wakefulness, and then he heard it. Scraping sounds from the kitchen. He was immediately entirely awake.

He twisted his head, the clock read 4:03. Before he'd fallen asleep, a little after one, he'd made sure to lock the door and windows. Not only that, but he'd taken Brandon's old bike chain from the cupboard and wrapped it around the handles on the fridge door, and fastened it shut. That ought to keep sleepy Ryan's hungry hands at bay, but—

The rattling came again, louder than before.

The fridge.

Ryan sat bolt upright, barely containing a scream.

Don't panic.

Whoever it is has been doing this for a while. If they were going to hurt him, they'd have done it already. Maybe it was an unhoused person who just needed food, but...how the fuck were they getting in? Ryan's eyes darted around the room for something to grab that might make him look a little more threatening than the six-foot mass of undefined skin and bones that he was and failed.

Fucking minimalism.

Ryan wriggled his way to the edge of the bed and stood as quietly as possible. His bedroom door was open just a little, enough so that when he crept close, he didn't have to open it to peek through into the open plan living area and kitchen.

There was a low, squelching grunt from somewhere in the darkness.

Ryan wondered if the intruder had somehow gotten into the fridge and was guzzling food.

A responding grunt came, high and crackling, almost like frog song.

It sent a shiver over Ryan's skin.

There were two of them, but what was wrong with their voices?

Swallowing, Ryan held his breath and eased open the door, peering into the dark. His eyes slid around the room, searching, and finding nothing.

A car passed on the street. Even here on the third floor, its lights strobed the room faintly. That was when he saw them.

Standing by the counter, no taller than his knees, were two creatures.

They were nobbled little things; small heads, bulbous and hairless, and the angles of their bones were visible through their skin, which looked like mouldy leather. Dark little eyes glittered close together in the centre of their faces, and small pointed teeth flashed as they grunted softly to each other.

A scream formed in Ryan's throat, and he forced it back down, terrified of alerting them to his presence. He needed to get his phone. To get a photograph of them or call the police. He took one slow step back, and a traitorous floorboard creaked.

Both sets of black eyes flashed immediately to the open doorway.

Ryan was already slamming it shut, his heart hammering in his chest as he flung his body against it. There were no locks in here, so he dropped to his knees and curled himself into a ball to use his body as a doorstop. His breath was as hard to catch as if he'd run a mile, and he clutched his legs as he listened to the scrabble of claws across the wooden floor outside.

~

I'M CALLING DOCTOR WALTERS.

MOTHRA

I'm fine.

RYAN

RYAN U CALLED THE POLICE BECAUSE YOU THOUGHT YOU HAD BOGLINS IN YOUR APARTMENT.

MOTHRA

I said goblins, Mom. But I already have an appointment with Dr Walters this week. I made it myself.

RYAN

U SHOULD CALL BRANDON.

MOTHRA

We broke up, Mom.

RYAN

HE STILL LOVES U.

MOTHRA

He has a new boyfriend already.

RYAN

DON'T EAT ANY CHEESE BEFORE BED TONIGHT. SHARON JUST TOLD ME IT MAKES YOUR DREAMS FUNNY.

MOTHRA

Okay, Mom. Thanks for that.

RYAN

DON'T THANK ME, THANK SHARON.

MOTHRA

~

RYAN WAS EXHAUSTED.

Anxiety induced hallucinations, Doctor Walters had said.

She'd made some changes to his prescription, but he'd have to go out to pick up the pills, and he barely dared to leave his bedroom.

He'd rushed into the kitchen around noon to grab some things out of the cupboard. Chips, cookies, and any other crap he dared before bolting back to his room with the biggest kitchen knife and one of the chairs from the dining table to use as a wedge under his doorknob. Last night, he'd huddled against the door until the sun rose. He daren't even move to his bedside table to grab his phone and leave the door free to be pushed open, in case those things got in. In the morning, he'd called the police. A fat lot of good *that* had done. He knew Doctor Walters was probably right. Fuck, his mom was probably right. His anxiety had gotten worse since Brandon left, and this isolation wasn't helping anything.

That night, he wedged the door shut with the chair just in

case and huddled in his bedclothes on the floor beside it. He lay cocooned in his comforter, thumbing through his phone until he inevitably circled the drain of old photos of him and Brandon and eventually fell asleep.

A FAINT SCRATCHING sound awoke him.

The moon peeked from high in the gap of the curtains.

Something was scratching against the outside of the door, like the tip of a thumbtack being slowly dragged across the lacquered wood right beside his head.

Ryan swallowed. Every fibre of his being vibrated with terror. "G...go away."

There was silence for a moment, and then...

"Ooooooooo!" a gargling voice mocked, followed by a throaty cackle. A heavy thump on the wood rattled the door.

"I'm calling the police." Ryan cried.

There was more scratching, harder now. Angrier.

Ryan thumbed his phone to life, pressing it to his ear as it rang.

"Police, what's your emergency?" a woman said politely.

"I'm... I'm trapped in my bedroom. Something..." Ryan shook his head, no, they wouldn't listen to that—they hadn't last time. "Someone's trying to get me."

There was a long pause.

"Sir, this number has been flagged for inauthentic calls."

Ryan's breath caught in his throat. The things outside the door were chuckling again.

"Please!" he cried. "You have to believe me. They're trying to get me."

There was another long pause, followed by a click and the sound of a dial-tone that felt closer to a flatline on life-support.

Ryan moved his phone away from his ear and stared at the screen.

They hung up.

His hands shaking, he did the only thing he could think of.

He called Brandon.

RYAN BLINKED SLEEPILY. He must have drifted off again. His head felt thick and foggy. Brandon was sitting beside him. Well, on the chair beside the bed, at least. Brandon had grown his beard out; he'd never done that for Ryan when he asked. The salt-and-pepper looked so sexy with his clean buzz cut hair. His flinty blue eyes were fixed on Ryan with... not concern. Was that pity?

"I can't stay anymore, Ryan. Your father's outside in the car. He shouldn't be out of the house, what with his condition," his mother was saying from the doorway.

That's right. They'd come. They'd all come.

Well, Brandon had arrived first, half asleep and in his sweatpants and T-shirt, mussed and smelling of sleep. His mother had materialised a few hours later, having taken the opportunity to break isolation to ensure she had a full face of makeup on and one of her nicest frocks.

"I love you, Ryan, but you really must get better. I'll get your room ready, and you'll be back with us by the end of the week." She waved sadly with one hand, then blew a kiss to Brandon.

Brandon gave her a tired wave.

Ryan's mother shot him a wink before she disappeared down the hall.

Ryan's eyes wandered down from where she'd stood, to

the open bedroom door. He gazed vaguely at the deep gouges on the panel.

There was a loud bang as the front door slammed shut.

"You know Ryan, I really thought you were above this kind of behaviour," Brandon grumbled. "Scratching up doors with a kitchen knife? Making up stories to get attention? It's just...selfish."

Ryan stared at him, numbly.

"And on my birthday? Really?" Brandon scowled, and folded his arms so that his biceps flexed the way Ryan always liked.

"What?" Ryan asked thickly.

Brandon stared at him disdainfully, before letting out a huffed breath and reaching over to the bedside table. "Look, just take the pills Doctor Walters left. She said you needed sleep more than anything, then...maybe we can talk. When this is all settled down, I mean." He swallowed. "I broke up with Andy. I...let's just talk later, okay?"

Ryan stared at him.

Doctor Walters had been here?

Yes. That's right. She'd given him a shot of something. Said he needed rest.

He nodded groggily. "Okay."

Brandon smiled. It wasn't his old smile, it was thin and sad, but it was something.

He leaned forward with the pill cup, and Ryan opened his mouth obediently for Brandon to tip them in, then took a big mouthful of water.

Ryan sunk back into his pillow, closing his eyes. "Tomorrow?" he repeated softly.

There was a moment's pause before Brandon replied. "Tomorrow."

~

RYAN EMERGED from sleep like a man emerging from the deep dark depths of a bottomless pool. It clung to him hungrily, a void desperate to swallow him back up. He clung to wakefulness, clawing his way through the drowsy fog. His head felt thick, but he felt...better. Calmer. He blinked sleepily. It was dark. He stretched his arms, almost expecting to feel Brandon nestled beside him, but found only the empty sheets. He remembered his last words with a smile.

Tomorrow.

Sleepily, Ryan tilted his head.

The chair beside him was empty, but something glittered in the darkness.

Ryan's eyes shifted to find it.

To find them.

The strange creatures stood close to his bed, watching him. Their dark beady eyes glittered cruelly, and their small mouths were crooked with malevolent smiles showing jagged little teeth. Only, there weren't two of them this time. There were more. So many more, standing all around his bed.

Their clawed feet scratched on the wooded floor as they moved toward him.

Ryan screamed.

BRANDON AWOKE WITH A START. "RYAN?" His voice was hoarse with sleep.

Silence.

Brandon groaned, scooting to the edge of the bed, and trying to work the crick out of his neck. He'd fallen asleep sitting up against the damned headboard, his phone in his lap. He thumbed the screen to life.

IS HE BACK YET?

RY'S MOM

Brandon thumbed in a negative response and set the phone down beside him. It felt fucked up being in their old apartment without Ryan, but also *right*. What didn't feel right was that Ryan was missing. He never should have left him. The hundredth vision of Ryan huddled in some alley, confused, shivering and alone, made Brandon curse himself again. The police wouldn't even listen until it had been twenty-four hours, so he'd promised Ryan's mother that he'd wait here in case he came home. He'd even dozed off with the door unlocked since Ryan's keys had been left on the counter and he didn't want to lock him out.

Something scraped in the next room.

Brandon sat bolt upright.

"Ry, is that you?" he croaked, standing, and rushing to the door. Brandon dashed into the living area, his eyes desperately searching in the dark for some sign of him, his heart teetering at the edge of a cliff between relief and disappointment. "Baby? Are you here?"

Something scraped above, like someone moving a chair in an apartment upstairs.

Except...this was the loft.

Brandon looked up.

One of the square ceiling boards was pulled aside. Brandon hadn't noticed that before.

Had Ryan been having some maintenance done?

Slowly, it shifted further, revealing the darkness within. The darkest darkness he'd ever seen.

"Ryan?" Brandon murmured weakly.

Glittering eyes shone from the void, and then, they were upon him.

7

FIRST, WE PRACTICE TO DECEIVE

The man was watching her.

Alice sipped her cocktail, relishing the cleansing combination of vodka and Acqua Bianca. He was handsome, at least; a boyish smile and flop of dark hair constantly threatening to cover one sparkling, cornflower blue eye. His friend laughed obnoxiously, braying like a donkey with pink ears and nicotine-stained teeth. His suit was cheaper than her admirer's—poorly fitted and pewter, uncouth beside the snug, deep charcoal of the one that would be hers.

Hers.

She was calling him that already?

They hadn't even spoken.

She felt a flush of heat as he looked at her again. He was growing bolder.

His eyes travelled down her body appraisingly.

Alice always wore a jacket when she was in public and favoured high-necked garments, but she relished in the elegance of her litheness and its subtle suggestion of her athleticism and power. She favoured quality materials, especially silks, that hung off her just so, accentuating her grace.

Alice risked a smile, coy and playful, toward her admirer. She was alone after all and didn't plan to leave that way.

The handsome man leaned close to his wretched friend and whispered something. His friend's eyes darted in her direction, skittering away just as quickly. The smirk on the red-eared man's face was ugly as he replied, before Alice's admirer moved toward her.

~

HIS NAME WAS KEVIN. She liked that. Simple, masculine, traditional.

She knew before he even said hello that no one would get him as hard as he was for himself. Still, at least he was trying to convince her—even if he kept getting distracted by his reflection in the mirror beside her like an overgrown budgerigar.

He flashed those perfect teeth and winked at her.

She wasn't exactly sure why he was smiling. She hadn't been listening to the last thing he said, but it certainly hadn't been funny.

Better play it safe.

She responded with a tinkling laugh. Enough to let him know she thought he was hilarious, but not so much as to sound like his donkey friend.

"So, babe, why are you here all alone?" Kevin asked.

"Oh, I wasn't supposed to be." The lie came easily, and others flowed in its wake. "I was meeting friends, but I just got a text telling me they got mugged on their way here. They're fine, a bit shaken up, but they've gone home. I thought I'd have one drink and try to have at least a little fun before I do the same."

Kevin's thick, dark brows knitted, but the smile didn't

drift far from his pretty lips. "I'm sorry to hear that. I guess it was fate, though, since now you're here with me."

Alice allowed herself a small smile and answered shyly, "Maybe it is."

Fate didn't have to be an accident. She was becoming more confident that he was the one she was looking for.

"The streets are dangerous nowadays, no telling what's lurking around the corner; it's a hard time to be a beautiful woman. That said, it's dangerous to be around a beautiful woman, too. So, I'm not sure who's in more danger right now, you or me." Kevin quirked an eyebrow seductively.

She could tell by the sparkle in his eyes that this was his best line. Her laugh was genuine. Perhaps he would realise later how funny what he'd just said was.

"Do you have any plans for the evening?" Alice's eyes drifted to his obnoxious friend, who was now talking loudly on his phone.

"Oh, I was just out with one of the boys. Plans change, though. Right now, I think I'll stick around you as long as you'll have me."

"I'd love to have you," Alice purred innocently.

Kevin's eyes shone.

"Can I buy you another drink, babe?" He gestured to her now empty glass. "What are you having?"

"That's so kind," she said, leaning forward to put her hand on his. It was large and warm, full of life. "A vodka stinger."

Kevin smirked, raising his eyebrows. "Classy lady. I've never even heard of that before."

"Do you mind if I pop to the ladies' room?"

"Of course not, babe." He grinned.

The flash in his eyes told her she had him.

She'd heard the rumours of someone matching his description frequenting this bar amongst others, but this was her fifth attempt, and she'd been growing bored. But finally, he'd stepped right into her web.

~

HIS DOSING WAS QUITE EXCELLENT.

He'd given her just the right amount, she could taste it. Ketamine, from the slightly increased bitterness to her drink. No human palate could have identified it, just enough to make someone a little more light-headed than they ought to be. As though this were their sixth drink rather than second. Make them more suggestible and relaxed. Not enough to raise the suspicions of the bar staff before he led them away. Alice allowed her eyes to become heavy and lidded as she sipped, her smile broad and close-lipped.

"What do you say you let me take you home, babe? Don't want you getting in trouble like your friends did," Kevin suggested.

Alice nodded dozily.

When she stood, she made sure to stumble against him. She didn't want to overdo it, just stepping into his space and resting against him unsteadily. She smelled the heady notes of his expensive aftershave and the beer on his breath, but also caught the sharp note of excitement in his scent, not sexual in the slightest. Closer to a predator hunting its prey, growing as near as it dared before it was detected. This man wasn't searching for pleasure, just business.

Good.

"Shall we get a cab?" She smiled.

~

THE SOFT SWELL of the voluptuous couch embraced Alice's body as she dropped bonelessly onto it. She allowed her arms and legs to fall akimbo, like a puppet with its strings cut. The door closed loudly, but she could tell he was still here. She wondered when Kevin had first done this. The records she had found went back almost three years, but his deviance likely began before.

She didn't need to wonder why he did it because she knew.

His scent was full of growing excitement and anticipation, as well as a rapidly blossoming sense of power.

She stretched languidly, like a vulnerable napping kitten.

His footfalls grew closer.

"Not great at handling your alcohol, huh, babe?" Kevin said.

She could hear the smirk in his voice.

"I'm just exhausted." She cracked her eyes and smiled. Why not toy with him a little?

Surprise and disappointment flickered in his eyes. "Can I, uh...get you a drink of water?"

"Please." She waved her hand toward the kitchenette. "There're bottles in the fridge."

She shut her eyes again and listened as he opened the fridge and removed a bottle, opening it on the countertop. Then she heard the faint sound of something else being unscrewed before he added it to her drink.

His breath hitched, and his scent danced on the edge of fear.

She smiled.

Then he was back. Sitting at Alice's feet, his eyes shining in the moonlight cast through the open blinds. He really was quite pretty.

"Thank you," Alice said softly, sitting up with feigned difficulty. She reached out and took the bottle with both hands.

"No worries." Kevin grinned. "Mind if I use your bathroom?"

"Not at all. Down the hall, first door on the right."

As he stood, Alice lifted the bottle to her lips and caught the scent of his chosen venom again. It was a pathetic poison, but this much may dull even her senses. Once she heard the bathroom door close behind him, she sprung silently to her feet and darted across the room to tip most of it down the sink. Quickly, she moved back to the couch, lying as she had before and allowing her arm holding the bottle to droop, fingertips touching the wooden floor. She let the bottle slip from her grip with a light thunk, and the dregs of its contents pooled around it.

A few moments later, the bathroom door opened again.

Alice closed her eyes and evened her breathing.

"Well, looks like someone is a thirsty girl," he whispered.

Alice struggled not to smile. She was supposed to be unconscious after all, but she really loved it when they said such creepy things. It made her feel so vindicated.

He moved so carefully that if not for his heartbeat, she'd barely have known he was there.

His fingers touched lightly at her throat, testing her pulse, before brushing back a strand of her dark silky hair from her forehead.

Just checking his wares.

His weight settled beside her as he sat on the edge of the couch.

She allowed her eyes to open just a little and found he'd pulled out his phone, his fingers moving against the screen. The large vessel in his neck throbbed, and she licked her lips. As his eyes remained fixed on his screen, she smoothly sat up behind him.

He gave a start when her lips met his flesh. Her teeth parted, and her tongue tasted stale aftershave and a light film of sweat. Before he had time to move or make a sound, two dark barbs punched down from Alice's gums, from high behind her top lip. They pierced his flesh smoothly before retracting, and the metallic taste of blood spread on her tongue. Her venom did not need a vein, but it found one.

Kevin let out a strangled whine as her poison surged to his heart. His body spasmed, then stiffened, his phone slipped from his fingers and clattered on the floorboards.

Alice laughed throatily, slipping from behind him and easing him into her place.

Kevin's eyes bulged, his jaw clenched, and spittle foamed at his lips.

Not so pretty now.

Smoothly, Alice picked up his phone and swept a finger across the screen, revealing his truths. The message he'd been typing to an unsaved number had not yet been sent. The corner of her mouth lifted in a smirk.

> Got another. Easy pickings. Come for collection. K.

Similar messages came before it, as she'd hoped. She'd found the one. She wondered how many of Kevin's colleagues would turn up if she pressed send.

Why not make it a party?

But first...

Alice slipped off her jacket, then unbuttoned her blouse smoothly. She tilted her head, parting the silk from her skin. "Not great at handling your alcohol, huh, babe?"

Kevin's eyes moved, the only part of him that could now, fixing on her body. Her beautiful black chitinous body that glittered in the moonlight. The pale flesh of her collarbones fused into a beautiful, dusky exoskeleton following the swell of her breasts and hips.

His eyes met hers again, bloodshot, and leaking tears.

He'd had no sexual interest in her at all, at least not for himself. It hadn't bothered her—Alice found no pleasure in men. Still, the horror that filled his eyes washed over her like a potent aphrodisiac.

No, more like an appetiser.

Smiling, Alice stretched her arms. All of them.

Eight spindling onyx appendages untucked from her back, each one longer than the fleshy pair before them, nobbled at their joints.

A low keening wail escaped Kevin.

Alice smiled. "Hush now. Please, take this time to remember how many people you've sold into misery. How many promising futures you've snuffed and lives you've torn apart? How could you ever have thought it would end well for you? This is what you deserve. What you have earned. More than, in fact."

Yes. She would send the message when she was done with him. They'd keep well enough wrapped up, and she needed them all.

Two of her limbs rubbed together, making a low humming sound.

Kevin was gurgling, his face growing purple. Whether he was drowning in saliva or choking on his tongue, she didn't care. He'd still be fresh enough.

The beautiful scuttling that filled the hallway flooded her heart with joy and brought a rapturous smile to her face. "You really should have treated us better. Each life you spoiled is a wonder, and each soul, a treasured sister, son...or mother."

The first of her children sprung onto the top of the couch, still just a bulbous abdomen with long limbs and a snapping maw. It leapt on Kevin greedily, its fangs sinking into his cheek.

More followed, falling over each other in their haste to get their meal, swarming his stiff body, unable to even scream.

Alice smiled and joined her children for dinner.

8

NO PLACE LIKE HOME

PART THREE

The sun hung low in the sky when Daniel finally plucked up the courage to make his way to the groundskeeper's cottage. He clutched a plate holding a very sorry looking and slightly soggy banana bread to his chest. He was a barely passable cook, but Knud seemed to enjoy baking, so this seemed a suitable peace offering to make.

It filled Daniel with a strange excitement, visiting this place he'd always been told not to go, to see a monster, no less. A monster that wore colourful trousers, cried quite a lot, and enjoyed housekeeping, but still.

The big door's red paint was flaking off, but its small round window was clean. Daniel's heart skipped at the sound of his knuckles rapping on the door, and in the brief moments that passed before it opened, Daniel considered running away five times.

Knud had to stoop to peer below the lintel. His red eyes narrowed beneath his bushy brows. He wore canary yellow trousers today, belted with thick rope beneath his round furry belly. He stared at Daniel thoughtfully, his mouth ajar, revealing the sharp teeth between the two tusk-like incisors jutting from behind his lower lip.

"Uh...hello, Knud. I came to apologise. And to thank you," Daniel croaked.

The monster's eyes travelled down to the miserable banana bread.

"I didn't mean to hurt you before. You just frightened me, and I reacted badly," Daniel said.

Knud blinked, and his eyes found their way back to Daniel's.

"I made this for you." Daniel thrusted his offering out before him.

One of Knud's massive hands gently plucked the plate away. Slowly, he lifted it and took a deep sniff then looked at Daniel, his red eyes slightly watery, and smiled. His voice was a low growl that sent chills up Daniel's spine.

"Thank you. Come in?"

Daniel, in too far to turn back now, nodded, and followed the monster into its lair.

KNUD'S COTTAGE was painstakingly clean, and yet, a stale scent lingered. An earthy musk with a biting edge that wasn't entirely unpleasant. Small pots of succulents lined almost every possible surface, and a picture sat on the bedside table of Daniel's aunt and uncle. A gigantic bed took up most of the building, but there was a round table set by a small stove and wooden countertop. Everything but the bed seemed children's play furniture beside Knud. Daniel took a seat at the table as the monster lumbered over to the small kitchen space.

"Your home is...lovely." Daniel almost managed to sound casual.

Knud took some plates from a stack and placed a tin kettle on the stove.

"Not real home." Knud grunted deeply. "Just stay here when you comes."

Daniel's eyes widened. "You normally live in the house?"

Knud nodded, one of his horns nearly scraping the roof.

"You and Aunt Bea were friends?" Daniel asked.

Knud looked very sad for a moment and sniffled.

Daniel feared he might start crying again.

"When Knud small, he was left on moors with note saying Knud's father demon and mother did not want. Knud evil curse baby. Mumbea found Knud and brought him home. Mumbea and Papa Tony could not have baby. Mumbea said Knud was gift, not curse."

Daniel stared in disbelief. Mumbea and Papa Tony? For a moment, he felt almost like he hadn't known them at all. Then, he imagined Uncle Tony dandling a massive hairy baby on his knee and Aunt Bea fussing over Knud, combing his mane of hair and kissing his broad nose. Daniel smiled. Actually, that sounded exactly like them.

"Knud got big fast and love helping. Mumbea love being helped, and Knud love Mumbea. Cleaning Knud's favourite but cooking fun too. When Daniel come to stay, Knud hide in old cottage, so Daniel not tell. Knud comes in night instead, to cook and clean, and have breakfast with Mumbea."

Daniel watched as a dreamy smile formed on Knud's face as his deep, rumbling voice grew higher in excitement. It seemed the monster was happy that Daniel had visited today; Daniel found himself smiling, too.

Knud took a bread knife from the counter that looked tiny in his giant hand and cut into the pitiful-looking banana bread.

"I'm sorry for your loss, Knud. I'm glad that Aunt Bea and Uncle Tony took care of you," Daniel said.

Knud sniffled once more.

Whatever Knud was, he had a kind heart. There was no denying he wasn't human and was quite terrifying, but he wasn't evil.

Knud turned and set two dinner plates on the table, Daniel's with a decent slice of cake, and Knud's with half of the soggy loaf.

The kettle whistled.

Daniel cleared his throat. "Knud, did you do something to scare away my parents? The manor. It was...angry."

Knud's red eyes brightened with amusement. "A little bit Knud, but mostly manor. Manor loves Knud. It wants to help him like he helps it."

"The manor?" Daniel repeated numbly.

"Mumbea call it old magick," Knud rumbled. "Put love into a thing, and the thing come alive."

Daniel chewed on that. It sounded unreal, but he was currently having afternoon tea in a monster's cottage, so who was he to argue? "So, the manor, is it alive?"

Knud poured the boiling water into a purple teapot and cast Daniel a brief sympathetic look, as if he were missing something extremely obvious. "Everything alive, but not talking all the time."

Daniel stared at the cups Knud had set on the worktop, suddenly wondering if they might spring into a musical number.

"Old magick stronger now." Knud set the kettle back down. "Manor happy Daniel home."

Daniel chewed his lip. "Do you love this cottage too, Knud?"

Knud grunted as he picked up the teapot, pinching the

handle with one huge finger and thumb. He shook his gigantic head, his mane of hair ruffling. "No. Too small. No bath."

Daniel nodded, unsurprised. There was barely room for them both in here, and perhaps that explained the musty smell. "You..." Daniel struggled, clearing his throat. "You can come and live in the house, Knud. I mean, if you want to."

Knud slowly turned to look at Daniel, surprised.

"And you can have a bath, too. Today," Daniel added, smiling awkwardly.

Knud's mouth opened in a sharp-toothed grin, those two stubby tusks almost touching his broad nose.

Embarrassed, and still a little afraid, Daniel looked away, studying the low ceiling instead. The gouges and scuffs decorating the stone above were undoubtedly from Knud's horns.

The monster set the teacups gently on the table and sat down. The chair creaked beneath his vast body, and one massive canary yellow trousered leg came to rest against Daniel's.

This close, Daniel could feel the heat from his body. His scent, too, was more potent, and confirmed Daniel's suspicions about his need for a bath. He watched Knud pick up his slab of cake and take a long, nostril-flaring sniff, then bite it in half. He chewed thoughtfully and swallowed.

Knud's red eyes came to rest on Daniel's, and his face grew solemn. "Delicious."

Daniel looked away, abashed. Searching for a distraction, his eyes found Knud's bed, its pale sheets were carefully folded neater than Daniel ever managed his own. Placed on one pillow was something familiar. A blue chequered shirt far too small for Knud. Daniel's shirt. The one he'd arrived wearing and left soaked on the hallway floor. "Knud, why do you have my shirt?"

Knud twisted, looking toward the bed, his chair creaking

in protest. When he turned back to Daniel, his dusky cheeks were ruddy and coloured. Was he blushing?

"Knud took to clean, but...smell nice already." He blinked awkwardly.

Now Daniel felt his own cheeks colour.

The clothes I wore for twenty hours to travel in? Unlikely.

To distract himself, Daniel picked up a slice of the banana bread and took a careful bite. He grimaced and almost spat it out; it was without a doubt the most disgusting cake he had ever tasted. He'd completely forgotten the sugar.

Daniel had always wondered why Aunt Bea and Uncle Tony had such a huge bath, and now he knew.

It took a while to fill, and as it did, Daniel busied himself looking for bath salts. He pulled out an array of lavender oils and peppermint scrubs from the cupboards and came across a broad flat brush with soft bristles. He set everything on the side of the bath and turned the water into a bubbling concoction of steaming vapours and fragrances.

Once the bath was as full as he dared make it without risking it overflowing when its giant bather submerged, he switched off the tap and tested the water with his elbow. Perfect. Hopping to his feet, he went out to the landing where Knud towered awkwardly, his hands folded across his belly and eyes anxious.

"Okay, Knud, all ready for you." Daniel's smile came surprisingly easily, given the strange turn of events.

Knud nodded, moving his hands down.

Daniel stared blankly as Knud untied the rope at his waist before he jolted in realisation and spun around. "I'll, uh, just be in the office."

He heard Knud's trousers hit the ground.

Daniel paused as Knud's heavy footsteps padded into the bathroom. He didn't close the door, and there was a splashing of water as he got in, followed by a long, low, rumbling appreciative groan.

"Is it okay?" Daniel asked weakly.

"Yes, Daniel. Thank you." Knud rumbled.

"Good. I'll go then."

"Daniel?"

"Yes, Knud?"

Knud hesitated before his voice rumbled again. "Mumbea always help Knud wash."

Daniel felt his face drain of colour.

"What?"

"Knud has bits can't reach. Needs help."

"Oh...okay." Daniel choked as he turned around, heat rushing to his face until his head threatened to pop. "I'm, uh, I'm coming in, then?"

Knud grunted in placid agreement.

Daniel rounded the corner, finding Knud half-reclined, his eyes closed, and his lower half mercifully mostly submerged beneath the bubbles.

"Which part do you need help with?" Daniel asked.

Knud opened one red eye and looked at Daniel, then sat up. The bathwater lapped with a threatening splash, seeking to escape. "Back," he said simply, pointing with one thick finger.

Daniel awkwardly picked up the peppermint body scrub and popped it open, dolloping it on Knud's shoulders.

"Careful," Knud said in as close to a yelp as his baritone went. "Cold!"

"Sorry." Daniel winced, picking up the loofah.

Daniel had to get on his knees to find the right angle. Knud's back was already wet enough for him to form a lather, and he rubbed with the loofah in short circular movements. Beneath the fur, despite his belly, Knud's body was heavy with muscle.

Knud let out a low groan that pinked Daniel's cheeks as he scrubbed. He forced himself to focus on his task. The patches of water visible were already murky, but Knud smelled cleaner. Daniel picked up the brush and began carefully working it through the soft fur on Knud's back. It was fortunately not tangled, but was a little matted in parts, so he took great care not to pull. He became quite engrossed in this delicate work and was leaning over to work on a patch on Knud's far shoulder when it happened.

Knud's face was already close to Daniel's neck, but he leaned forward further still. His short, blunt horn pressed against Daniel's jaw, tilting his head away. Knud took a long sniff, his wide nose pressing against the sensitive flesh of Daniel's throat.

Daniel froze, almost dropping the brush into the water. His mind flashed back to the sniff Knud had given the banana bread before biting it clean in half.

Why is he sniffing me? Does he want to...eat me?

Daniel gulped, too startled to move, and felt a bead of sweat trickle down his back.

Knud took another long deep sniff, pressing his nose deeper into Daniel's throat, one of his tusk-like teeth pushed on Daniel's collarbone, and his hot exhaled breath set the flesh at his throat alight. The monster let out a low, rumbling groan.

Coming to his senses, Daniel jolted upright, knocking two of the soap bottles off the edge of the bath and clattering onto the floor as he did.

"I think I've got all the bits you can't manage, Knud." Daniel's voice quavered in time with his hammering heart.

Knud had a distant expression on his face, his eyes glassy as though drunk. He doesn't look hungry. He looks...

"You have enough towels to get dry when you've finished. I hope you enjoy being back in your bed," Daniel practically shouted as he staggered backward.

Something was happening beneath the bubbles between Knud's legs, threatening to push them aside indecently.

"Daniel," Knud said, dreamily.

The low rumble of Knud saying his name that way sent a warm shiver right through Daniel's bones.

Daniel turned and fled.

DANIEL COULDN'T SLEEP.

How could he, after the last few days?

He couldn't sleep, and he couldn't stop thinking about Knud.

He lay huddled in his sheets, staring at the clock's sallow face, trying to decide what to do, what to say, or at least what to think. One thing was for sure; he couldn't sell Greene Manor. This was his, and even more, it was Knud's. It was theirs. What was that Knud had said about old magic? It was stronger with Daniel here. Stronger with them both here. Together. Daniel was sure that he couldn't leave Knud alone, that much was obvious. What kept catching somewhere inside him, however, was an additional problem. He didn't *want* to.

The clock said it was a little past midnight when he heard it. The sobbing from down the hall sounded like rolling thunder.

Knud was weeping.

Daniel's heart clenched in his chest as he listened for

what felt like hours, but the clock promised was only minutes.

He couldn't bear to hear him so sad.

Daniel slipped from his covers and crept down the hall, wearing only his T-shirt and boxers. The old wooden floor, prone to loud creaks, stayed silent under his feet, as though the house itself encouraged his quiet passage. He knew which room was Knud's, even without the sobs coming from within. The place he used to visit and marvel at the size of the four-poster bed.

Daniel pushed open the door, which was already ajar, before Knud heard him.

Not that the door creaked, but Knud must have heard his breath or beating heart. The monster grew quiet, twisting to look at him, his wet red eyes shining in the darkness.

Daniel swallowed. He opened his mouth to speak, but then closed it again.

Slowly, he walked to the bed.

In a single motion, Daniel lifted the sheets and slipped beneath them.

Knud remained utterly motionless. Even his breath frozen in his chest, as if even the slightest movement may frighten Daniel away, like some small curious woodland animal.

Heart pounding, Daniel shimmied over and pressed his body against Knud's massive form, feeling his warm furry skin against his own. From the soft brush against his thighs, he realised Knud was naked. The smell of peppermint and lavender with the slightest musk of Knud welcomed him.

Knud let out a long rumbling breath, and Daniel felt Knud's face press against his forehead, wet with tears, before he took a long slow sniff, breathing him in.

Knud moved, his massive arms powerful enough to crush Daniel to a pulpy death instead wrapping around him and engulfing him gently, pulling him closer.

Daniel nestled against Knud's round belly, breathing him in return, and closed his eyes. He'd been gone from Greene Manor for too long, and now he knew he'd never leave again.

Because now he knew he was home.

THE END

ALSO BY RORY MICHAELSON

The Lesser Known Monsters Series

Lesser Known Monsters

The Bone Gate

The Torn Earth

The Little Book of Lesser Known Monsters

The LESSER KNOWN MONSTERS series is a dark queer fantasy featuring diverse characters on a found family adventure. Perfect for fans of horror and paranormal romance who seek LGBTQ+ heroes.

Being the chosen one isn't always a good thing.

Oscar Tundale is not a hero. Anxious, indecisive, and awkward, he can barely get through a normal day. Now he's about to find out monsters are real. Oscar's friends: brave, stubborn Zara, and hyperactive, paranoid Marcus, might help discover what hunts him, and unravel the truth about the handsome doctor he pines for. But only heroes can save the world, so maybe the best Oscar can hope for is to not end it by accident.

Please keep reading for a preview of the first chapters of ...

'Lesser Known Monsters.'

LESSER KNOWN MONSTERS

PREVIEW

LESSER KNOWN MONSTERS

RORY MICHAELSON

LESSER KNOWN

MONSTERS ®

"HELLO, CRICKET!"

EXCITARE

It is the eleventh of October, at four twenty-three in the morning. The weather in **London** is overcast with a temperature of nine degrees Celsius (forty-eight point two degrees Fahrenheit if you're into that sort of thing.) There has been mild precipitation; this *is* **England**, after all.

Oh, and **the world is ending**.

The world is ending, and it is due to the choices of a young man named **Oscar Tundale**. He is entirely average in many ways and less than average in more. This is the story of why the world is ending.

And how Oscar let it happen.

☙ I ❧
THE BLANKET MONSTER

"Oh, Oscar," Paige groaned. "You're about as much use as tits on a teapot."

A hedgehog in a condom factory.

A fart in a colander.

A cock flavoured lollipop.

If Oscar had learned one thing from Paige, it was how many interesting but not very useful things he was the human equivalent of. Though the last one didn't sound bad at all in his opinion.

"I'm sorry," Oscar rubbed at his eyes with his free hand. "I'll do it when I get back. Promise."

His sister sighed, her breath rasping in the earpiece of his phone. "Make sure you do. If they cut the electricity off, I'm not there to warm a bath up for you with the fucking kettle again."

"Sorry, Paige."

"Don't be sorry. You're always sorry! Just sort it out this time," she snapped. The hum of voices in the background was making it difficult to hear her now.

He heard someone call her name.

"Listen, Oscar, I've got to go. Some shit's kicking off. I'll call you later. We need to talk about something."

"Okay."

"And Oscar?"

"Yes?"

"Pay the bloody electricity bill."

"I will." The words were still leaving his mouth when the line disconnected with a blip in his ear. Oscar sighed, pushed his phone into his pocket, and looked up at the night sky.

So far as the London autumn sky was willing to disclose, it could have been seven at night or in the morning. As far as Oscar's bones and brain were willing to share, it was definitely around four o'clock in the morning. That was the point when the night shift always started to drag into monotonous delirium.

He took a moment, burying cold fingers into the hungry pockets of his threadbare pea coat. His old jacket had seen better days, but Oscar had a habit of wearing things until they fell apart. Besides, this jacket was perfect year-round if he added or subtracted layers underneath. What more could he ask for?

His breath misted the night.

Paige had been gone for three months, finally living the life she'd always dreamed of. He was happy for her. She'd worked hard, and when the offer for an internship at a big magazine in New York came through, her bags were half-packed before she even put the phone down. It meant Oscar had the apartment they shared all to himself. It was a little lonely sometimes, but he did have much more time to spend with Zara and Marcus, and he definitely spent a lot less time being scolded.

His phone buzzed in his pocket, and he inched it out carefully, just enough to peer at the screen but still protect his now warming fingers from the night's nipping chill.

Come back in Booboo. We got a new patient.

— ZARA

Oscar smiled tiredly and cast a glance up at the half-eaten moon, before making his way back into the hospital.

THURSDAY NIGHTS WERE USUALLY PRETTY slow, aside from the occasional toddler who found something exciting and dangerous to eat whilst their parents weren't looking. The Children's Assessment Unit had an otherwise steady stream of irritating coughs, nasty vomiting, or troubling fevers that kept it ticking along. When he got back to the Nurse's Station, the look on Zara's face told Oscar that the new patient in bed seven hadn't been admitted for eating their building blocks.

This time of night was usually the worst time for new admissions. Ripe for sighs, stoic and exhausted half-smiles, and the occasional sloppy mistake. Zara, however, was bouncing on her toes.

"What happened?" Oscar asked.

Zara's eyes flashed, the colour of freshly fallen autumn leaves. Her round face and golden-brown skin practically glowed under the dimmed lighting, usually bright and hostile on the day shift.

This is not how someone should look at this hour.

"A new patient just came in." She tucked her hair behind her ear. Finishing at her jaw, it was streaked with a vivid teal at the moment and was shaved short at her right temple to show a row of gold piercings in her ear. "No parents with her and she's been cut."

Oscar frowned. "Like...she cut herself on something?"

"No, like someone cut her. Pretty bad, apparently. The on-call surgeon patched her up in Emergency, but she might have to be operated on tonight."

"Oh my God." Oscar's eyes widened. "Who would do that to a child?"

"Some sicko. Probably one of the parents." Zara's eyes sparkled angrily.

Oscar flinched. Zara's heart was kind, but as one of the most senior nurses on the unit, she was a force to be reckoned with if a child needed her. She would stop at nothing to help her patients. Oscar had nowhere near her qualifications or responsibilities and often found himself watching her with awe. He'd seen her face down more arrogant junior doctors than he could count.

"Who's on call tonight?" Oscar swallowed, dreading the reply.

A flash of concern passed across Zara's face, but she quickly replaced it with a forced smile. "Ocampo." She tried to make the name sound as gentle as she could manage, but Oscar's face twitched anyway. "Don't worry," Zara said quickly. "I'll try and keep her away from you."

"How are you going to do that? By flirting?" Oscar grumbled.

Zara raised her hands innocently. "It's totally a professional crush. I mean she's an amazing doctor, and yeah, Ocampo is hot. That little pouty thing her mouth does when she's thinking. And how she always looks kind of *mean*, that's weirdly hot, too." Zara smiled, staring into space wistfully, then caught sight of Oscar's scowl. "Okay it's a professional crush first and a sexy crush second. But definitely in that order." She cleared her throat. "Anyway, we should, umm..."

"Should I go and do observations on the other patients?"

"Ah. Well..." Zara scrunched her eyes and shifted on her feet uncomfortably. "I actually kind of need you to go and sit with the new kid. She must be scared, and we don't have the staff to send a nurse to do it. She's all alone, Os."

Oscar's stomach dropped. *All alone?* "Really? But what about social work?"

Zara sighed. "They won't be here until the morning. The police called them when they dropped her off. They'll be back again tomorrow to try and take a statement. The girl wouldn't talk apparently, and they couldn't find her parents anywhere." Her eyes caught his for a moment, and he saw a flash of emotion.

Oh.

Oscar ran his hand through the messy chestnut mop that was his hair.

They left her. Just like...

He pushed the thought away firmly. "Are you sure it's okay?" Usually, his duties involved taking routine observations and serving out meals. Supervising a child who'd just been assaulted wasn't something he'd done before.

"Just press the buzzer if you need me, Booboo." Zara reached over and squeezed his shoulder, giving him an encouraging smile. "I know you'll do great."

OSCAR'S FINGERS traced the door handle as he worried his lip.

What should I say? Is there something that might help? Something that might have helped...me?

Finally steeling himself, he decided to give a gentle knock before pushing the door open. "Uh...hello?" He made his voice as soft as possible as he peeked around the edge.

The small en suite's fluorescent light glared through the half-closed door casting a dull glow over the attached bedroom. On the bed, a pair of large dark eyes peered at him from amongst a bundle of hospital linen. The sheets were pulled up to nearly completely cover the new patient, only owlish eyes and a tangle of raven hair standing out in the darkness.

"Hi," Oscar said nervously, aware of the tremor in his voice as he slid through the narrowly opened doorway. "I'm Oscar Tundale, one of the Health Care Assistants. Zara asked me to come and sit with you. Is that okay?"

The girl stared back at him in muted silence for a long moment, then finally gave him a single uncertain nod.

"Your name's Nina?" Oscar made his way toward the tall backed chair at the bedside.

The bundle of blankets, hair, and large dark eyes jiggled again in the affirmative.

Oscar sat down, his knee knocking painfully against the side of the bed as he did. The clatter and Oscar's gasp of pain made the little girl recoil inside her swaddle of sheets.

"I'm sorry. Are you okay?" The words tumbled out of Oscar's mouth. "Does it hurt? I can ask Zara if you need some medicine."

The bundle shook side to side in a motion that he guessed was a no.

Oscar relaxed a little and felt some of the tension leave his smile. "It's very late. Aren't you sleepy?"

There was another shake side to side for 'no.'

"Well, I suppose blanket monsters don't get tired easily. This is the first time I've really met one myself, though." Oscar tried to grin encouragingly.

The blankets inched back, revealing the girl inside. The first thing Oscar thought was that she looked much younger than he had expected, maybe only eight or nine years old.

This thought was chased by the horror that anyone would ever raise a hand to harm her. Her skin was a sandy brown, and her eyes almost as black as her hair, with round, cherubic cheeks and the sweetest bashful smile.

Oscar formed his mouth into a perfect 'O' and widened his eyes. "But you're not a blanket monster at all!" He raised his voice in mock surprise. "You're a little girl!"

The girl nodded, firmly folding her arms and trying to pull a serious face that was somewhat ruined by the grin she was unable to smother.

"That's probably why I wasn't scared. I'm not very brave, so if I met a real blanket monster, I'd just run away."

Nina gave him a shy smile and started to wriggle back into her blankets. As she moved to pull them about her, she suddenly stiffened in pain and let out a low squeak.

"Oh." Oscar reached out, but the girl flinched away from his touch, looking at him fearfully. Quickly, Oscar pulled his hand back, placing it on the edge of the bed instead. "Are you okay?"

Nina looked at him with dark teary eyes, her bottom lip trembling.

"I'm sure you are. You're not like me," Oscar tried to make his voice light and playful again. "You're super brave. I bet if you saw a blanket monster, you wouldn't even run away. I bet if you saw *any* monsters, you wouldn't run away, would you?!"

Her large dark eyes shone like pools of bitter chocolate, and Oscar felt like his heart was being squeezed.

This girl...

The door creaked open slowly, and Nina jumped. Her small, cool fingers shot out and latched onto Oscar's hand.

"Hey there. How are you two getting on?" Zara beamed, peering around the door.

Nina's grip relaxed slightly.

"I came to bring you some medicine. Doctor Ocampo just called to let me know she's nearly here." Her eyes took in Nina's hand clutching at Oscar's, and she gave him an encouraging smile. "Do you think I could check your dressings while I'm in here?"

Nina shot an anxious look at Oscar.

"Oscar can stay. You can squeeze his hand if it hurts." Zara winked, setting the tray of medicines down.

The little girl looked back at Zara and nodded tentatively.

Zara held out a translucent purple syringe cloudy with thick sticky medicine. The girl surprised Oscar by leaning forward and quietly taking the medication from Zara and popping it between her teeth, gulping down the substance inside without any fuss.

Instead of being surprised, Zara used the opportunity to ease the blankets wrapped around the girl from her back and gently pull her long hair over her shoulder. The back of her gown was misshapen with the swell of bandages beneath. Oscar couldn't help but let out a gasp when Zara unknotted the ties and let the fabric slide free. Most of the girl's back was covered in thick pressure dressings. Several patches were dark with dried blood.

Who would do this to a little girl?

Oscar caught a glimpse of Nina's large, dark eyes fixed on his face, and realised the expression she must have seen. He forced the shock down into his guts and plastered on what he hoped was a reassuring smile. "Those bandages look really cool, Nina," he said weakly.

The girl gave him a doubtful look.

"They're all intact and dry," Zara said, shifting the gown back into place. "Hopefully we will be able to let you rest for the rest of the night."

There was a rhythmic clopping from the hallway outside, gradually getting louder.

The hairs on Oscar's arms raised, and ice ran down his spine. He recognised that sound well, and nothing good ever came of it. Not for him anyway.

"Oh. It sounds like Doctor Ocampo is here," Zara said with a forced airiness, avoiding Oscar's gaze.

Oscar wondered if this is how his own fake smile to Nina looked just moments ago. The feeling of unease settled into an unpleasant dread wriggling in his stomach.

Well, he thought resignedly, *it's too late to escape now*.

2
THE BAD MAN

There was an ever so delicate rap of knuckles against the door before it opened to admit Doctor Ocampo. She'd only been at the hospital for a year but already owned a formidable reputation. Zara had explained to Oscar that Doctor Ocampo was highly regarded across the medical community and could have chosen almost anywhere to work and named her price. She'd published a myriad of contentious and cutting-edge studies, and her employment caused an excited buzz amongst the existing medical team. After her arrival, that buzz had quickly escalated to a screeching cacophony of protests and dismay.

Excellence. She always expected excellence.

Only, her own standards seemed agonisingly far above everyone else's, and she had no qualms about letting them know it. Her reputation wasn't hurt by the fact that she cut such a striking figure either. Angular features, porcelain skin, and black hair like silk gathered in a bun at the nape of her neck. Tonight, she wore a sumptuous plum blazer over a sleek black dress. Her high-heeled pumps were such a pristine white, Oscar couldn't help but wonder if she took them off to go outside.

"Doctor Ocampo, thank you for coming so fast. I was just looking at Nina's dressings," Zara said smoothly.

Doctor Ocampo's dark eyes took in both the girl and Zara, before drifting toward Oscar, Nina's hand still clutched in his own. One immaculate eyebrow twitched, her thin lips pursed, and she smoothed her blazer as if the thing could fit her any better. She pulled short of open disdain, a pleasant surprise for Oscar. Doctor Ocampo never made any secret of how underwhelmed she was by his existence.

When Doctor Ocampo spoke, it was short, sharp, and precise. Decisive cuts of a surgical blade. "Hello Nina, I'm Doctor Ocampo." She flashed a smile just brief enough to serve its purpose. "I'd just like to have a look at your back if that's okay?"

The girl seemed hypnotised by Doctor Ocampo and gave her an awed nod.

"Excellent," Doctor Ocampo said crisply. "I'm going to need a dressing pack." Her dark eyes drifted to Oscar with expectancy.

"I can get it," Zara chirped.

"I'd prefer you to stay and take down the dressing, Zara." Doctor Ocampo's sharp voice softened for Zara. A honeyed scalpel for her.

"I'll fetch it," Oscar squeaked. He disentangled his fingers from Nina's and concentrated on not tripping over his own feet as he rushed to the door.

Oscar let out a tense breath as he let it close behind him.

He wasn't sure exactly what he had done wrong so far as Doctor Ocampo was concerned. He was convinced that, in her opinion, he just never did anything right.

His charting was messy.

His answers were slow.

His hands were clumsy whenever she asked him for help.

There was such a thing as a self-fulfilling prophecy, and this one was fuelled by the fact that Doctor Ocampo seemingly saw no value in him at all.

Oscar chided himself as he rushed down the dimmed corridor.

Just keep your head down and work harder.

Zara said he worried too much about what other people thought, and that's was what made him so anxious and indecisive. It was kind of a difficult obstacle to overcome, particularly when someone made their negative thoughts so clear. He could imagine Doctor Ocampo now, patting her freshly washed hands dry with a paper towel, the corner of her mouth curling with thinly veiled disdain that Oscar was taking so long for a simple task. He spun around the corner to the storeroom and collided bodily with something, or rather, someone.

Something between an instinctive apology and a shocked yelp burst out of Oscar's mouth even as he belatedly tried to slow down, step back, and stop all at once. His feet caught against one another, and he tumbled backwards. He would have fallen flat out on the dingy speckled laminate floor, but a pair of hands shot out and clutched him, one by the shoulder and one at his waist.

"Oh, God. I'm so sorry," Oscar blustered, struggling to regain his footing. "I'm...oh."

Pale grey eyes regarded him with concern. "Are you okay?"

Of course. Of all the people, it had to be him.

"I'm fine, thank you, Dmitri," Oscar managed breathily.

Dmitri ran a hand through his dark hair, tucking a few stray strands back behind his ear. He wasn't much taller than Oscar, but something just seemed more *solid* about him. A plump bottom lip weighed down a perfect cupid's bow, a nearly delicate nose, and a sharply angled jaw that seemed to have a permanent shadow of stubble. His intense stormy grey eyes fixed on Oscar from beneath thick dark brows in a way that made Oscar's knees feel like jelly.

"Good, I'm glad. I didn't mean to surprise you." His lips quirked in a charming half-smile.

Too handsome, Oscar thought numbly. *And the accent*.

His words curled like he was kissing them out of his mouth and they just wanted to go right back in. Oscar never felt quite so awkward as he did when he was speaking to this man. Not just because of what happened, but because standing beside him made Oscar all the more aware of his own flaws. The way he stood all gangly-limbed like one of those tufty haired Troll toys. His long arms and legs never quite seemed to get the memo of exactly what he wanted them to do, and he was so clumsy he usually had at least one good bruise on him at all times. That was why Zara had taken to calling him Booboo. He almost felt the urge to cover his face and hide his long, freckled nose and the small gap between his front teeth.

Instead, Oscar laughed awkwardly, willing the pink he knew would be blossoming around his ears to subside. "It's my fault, I was in a rush. Are you okay?"

Dmitri crinkled his eyes like he was confused by the question and shook his head. "Of course, I'm fine."

Why did he always have to smell so good? Clean, like citrus, but with a deep and smoky note. Like charred cedarwood.

Oscar tensed, realising Dmitri's hand was still on his shoulder, he was immediately conscious of every finger. He was suddenly sure they were burning through the thick fabric of his pale green uniform. He was still standing far too close; he could practically feel Dmitri's breath on his face.

Dmitri tilted his head curiously, eyes searching.

Oscar's stomach leapt, and he took a stumbling step

away, almost tripping over his own feet again. "So, can I help?" he slurred, his tongue seemingly too large for his own mouth.

For God's sake.

It was one date. One coffee. They hadn't even kissed, though Oscar had spent the whole hour watching Dmitri's lips move as he spoke, wondering how they would feel against his own. It ended quite abruptly, a glance at a phone and an apology for the need to rush off.

Then Dmitri never contacted him again.

Zara had been full of advice for that, as if she hadn't been the one to encourage him to go on the date in the first place. She didn't want to hear about how awkward Oscar felt now whenever the far too handsome doctor from the labs made an appearance on the ward.

Why is someone so intelligent allowed to look like that anyway?

"I'm here to see the new patient. To take photographs and swabs," Dmitri said softly.

"Oh, yes." Colour flooded Oscar's face.

Now? Why?!

Was every part of his body going to betray him? He needed to get away from here before blood started pouring from his nose, or his eyes popped out like a ridiculous cartoon character.

"She's in cubicle seven." He waved emphatically back in the direction he came from.

Dmitri gave a small smile and stepped past him.

Oscar, feeling like his bones were now half dissolved, practically slithered to the storeroom door a few feet away.

"Do you need any help?" Dmitri asked.

Oscar turned to see him still watching, brow slightly furrowed.

"No," Oscar replied far too quickly to be polite. "No, thank you," he added with a nervous grin. Dmitri chuckled, raising a hand in a motionless wave, before rounding the corner.

Oscar let the storeroom swallow him up, hoping that the ground might open up beneath him too if he wished hard enough. The door closed behind him, and he leaned back on it, feeling it cool against his back through his uniform. His heart rushed in his chest like it had somewhere to go and needed to get out. From the way his skin tingled, he was quite sure that if he took off his shirt now, he would see two handprints—one on his arm and one over his ribs.

He let out a deep breath and dropped his head back against the door with a loud hollow thunk.

IT TOOK a few moments more than it should have for Oscar to find the dressing packs in the cluttered storeroom. He checked them every day and should have been able to find them with his eyes closed. Still, the combination of Doctor Ocampo and Dmitri had undoubtedly caused some kind of short circuit in his brain. When he was nearly back to the room, he wondered if he'd been gone for much longer than he anticipated.

Doctor Ocampo was coming out of the cubicle when he approached. Her pale skin had taken on a slightly mottled tone, and her eyes flashed with bubbling rage.

"Sorry, Doctor Ocampo, I—" Oscar began.

Doctor Ocampo reared back like a snake about to strike, an expression of alarm on her face—or maybe surprise that he had the nerve to continue to exist. "What?" she spat, eyes flashing to the dressing pack in his hands. "Oh. Zara will see to that. I've had quite enough for one night." She waved a lithe hand in dismissal and stalked past him with an angry clicking of heels.

Curious and confused, Oscar pushed into the cubicle, where Zara was fussing over Nina, who wriggled and whimpered on the bed.

"What happened?" Oscar looked around the room, feeling both relief and disappointment that Dmitri was not there.

Zara shot him a significant look. "Labs came up to take a sample from the wound. Nina was frightened, and Doctor Ocampo got really mad and sent him away."

Oscar placed the dressing pack on the foot of the bed.

"Wow."

He was glad that he managed to avoid *that* situation at least, but it was difficult to imagine someone lashing out at Dmitri. He was always so placid and amiable. But then, Doctor Ocampo did seem to have excess venom that needed to be drained regularly.

Nina was coiling the blankets around her again, sobbing quietly.

Sighing, Zara stepped back and looked at the shaking bundle with worried eyes. "Listen, can you stay with her, Os? I'll go and get something to help her settle down."

"Okay." Oscar bit his lip, realising he sounded more confident than he felt, and made his way back to the chair by her bed.

The door banged shut behind Zara.

Oscar sat, tensely watching the whimpering blankets, struggling to find the right words.

She must be so scared. No one here to comfort her...I...what can I...

"Hey there, blanket monster," he said softly. "I thought you weren't really a blanket monster at all?" The words sounded limp even to him.

The bundle let out a little mewl.

"I'm sorry you were scared," Oscar said sadly. "The man

that came, he just wanted to help you. He wanted to make sure whoever did this to you didn't get away with it, and—"

A small cold hand darted out of the sheets and grabbed onto Oscar's wrist, short nails digging in and making him gasp in surprise. The bundle of covers slid down, and Nina's face appeared, large black eyes terrified and welling with tears.

"That man. It was him." Her small voice was strangled and full of woe.

"What?"

"That...that was the bad man."

ACKNOWLEDGMENTS

Writing is something I started to do purely for myself, so imagine my surprise when it became the thing that connected me deeply with others.

Jayme, the alpha, beta, and omega reader for this series; I couldn't have done any of this without you. Shimaira, creator of 'Team Knud' and all round biggest cheerleader for The Little Book of Lesser Known Monsters, thank you for all of your support. I will always be grateful to the writing community who uplifted and held me up when hard work and timing was not quite enough. And of course, special thanks to my partner, who empowers the chaotic tornado that is me to keep spinning and crushes my soul back into my body when required.

And thank *you*, the reader of my silly little monster books. I aim to use my words to carve out safe spaces for us in unexpected places for us to find respite, strength, or a moment of joy, so I hope you enjoy them.

ABOUT THE AUTHOR

Rory Michaelson is always doing too many things, and rarely the ones they ought to be. There're empty spaces on shelves where LGBTQIA+ and neurodivergent books belong, and Rory hopes to to help fill them.

PRAISE FOR

LESSER KNOWN MONSTERS

"Sparkling, innovative, and most importantly, fun. Everything you could want in a vast, twisty feat of characters and dark fantasy."
Adam Sass, award-winning author of Surrender Your Sons

"Dreamy prose, fully realised characters I couldn't help but fall in love with, and a storyline that is both thrilling and tender."
Jonny Garza Villa, author of Fifteen Hundred Miles from the Sun

"Good twists, good monsters, and all the heart of a true found family."
David Slayton, author of White Trash Warlock

"A wonderfully queer, riveting, and heartfelt found family adventure that shows even the most average person can save the world...or end it."
Jayme Bean, author of Untouched

www.ingramcontent.com/pod-product-compliance
Lightning Source LLC
Chambersburg PA
CBHW030601310726
48979CB00003B/524
* 9 7 8 1 8 3 8 1 6 6 0 8 3 *